Her heart r... ...... and her breath caught in her throat.

The man who entered the weak circle of light registered a barely discernable flicker of surprise, just as she suppressed one of her own. *Mark.* Instant recognition promised instant death if he blew her cover. Her fingers slipped around the grip of her pistol.

She raised a brow and offered him the ghost of a smile. He returned it, just a small quirk of his lips. Nice lips they were, too. She remembered them well. Their texture, their taste, their hunger that had fueled hers.

But one kiss, mind-blowing as it had been, did not provide a basis for putting her life in the man's hands now.

That killer body of his could be just that—the body of a killer.

Dear Reader,

What a great time I've had working on the MISSION: IMPASSIONED series! I do hope you've had the opportunity to read the four books preceding mine and will be as eager as I am to read Kathleen Creighton's finale next month. It has been a real privilege to participate in this project with such wonderfully talented writers who are terrific characters in their own right!

The plotting was a blast from the first day! One of my Special Ops operatives jumped the big pond to join the fun in Paris. Though Compass agent Renee's agenda proved different from Mark Alexander's, our Lazlo agent, she definitely plays well with others in every sense of the word.

Everyone should have at least one wild adventure in Paris and I hope you enjoy this one!

Happy reading!

Lyn Stone

Lyn Stone

KISS
OR KILL

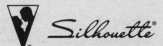

Romantic
SUSPENSE

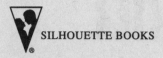 SILHOUETTE BOOKS

ISBN-13: 978-0-373-27558-8
ISBN-10:   0-373-27558-7

KISS OR KILL

Copyright © 2007 by Lynda Stone

This edition published by arrangement with Harlequin Books S.A.

® and TM are trademarks of Harlequin Books S.A., used under license.
Trademarks indicated with ® are registered in the United States Patent
and Trademark Office, the Canadian Trade Marks Office and in other
countries.

Visit Silhouette Books at www.eHarlequin.com

Printed in U.S.A.

Books by Lyn Stone

Silhouette Romantic Suspense

Beauty and the Badge #952
Live-in Lover #1055
A Royal Murder #1172
In Harm's Way #1193
*Down to the Wire #1281
*Against the Wall #1295
*Under the Gun #1330
*Straight Through the Heart #1408
*From Mission to Marriage #1444
*Special Agent's Seduction #1449
Kiss or Kill #1488

*Special Ops

LYN STONE

is a former artist who developed an early and avid interest in criminology while helping her husband study for his degree. His subsequent career in counterintelligence and contacts in the field provided a built-in source for research in writing suspense. Their long and happy marriage provided firsthand knowledge of happily-ever-afters.

This one is for my Hotlanta buddy, Deb Martin.

Prologue

London, 1991

"Son, put down the book. Get up quietly and do exactly as I say."

The unusual, low-voiced command grabbed Mark's attention and he glanced up. The television blared Cagney's snarling voice in an old American gangster movie his father had been watching. Totally disinterested, Mark had been devouring the last chapter of a current mystery novel. "What?"

His father snatched the book from his hand and threw it on the floor. "Crawl into the cupboard there. Hurry."

Mark laughed, watching as his dad opened the

cabinet and raked out the pillow and blanket kept there for anyone bunking on the couch. "I'm thirteen now, not three! I won't fit." His lanky, all-knees-and-elbows build caused enough laughs as it was without the old man making jokes about it.

His dad grasped his arm. "Get in there. *Now!* Fold yourself up, close the door and don't move a hair no matter what! Do not come out, do you hear, Mark? Can you follow orders or not?"

Mark started to argue, but noted the alertness in his father's expression, felt the incredible tension in the strong fingers locked around his arm. This was no joke. "Dad, what's wrong?" he whispered.

"A break-in, I think," his father answered, barely audible above the shoot-'em-up on television. He pushed Mark into the enclosure, roughly tucking in one big socked foot that stuck out oddly. "Stay there. I can't be worried for your safety, too. Do I have your word?"

"Yes! Call the police, Dad!" Mark gasped. His neck was bent at an unnatural angle and he felt like a freaking contortionist.

"I will. Do not move until I come back for you and tell you it's safe." His eyes met Mark's before he shut the door. In them Mark saw fear, something he had never in any way associated with his dad. The man was courage itself, everyone knew that.

Mark waited for what seemed forever, wincing at the jarring volume of the noisy telly just above him. It eclipsed all other sounds. He couldn't stand not knowing what was happening. It couldn't hurt to ease the door open a mere crack. Half an inch only, and he wouldn't even have to move his head to see out.

Immediately he saw a silhouette moving into the lounge from the kitchen. He held his breath. The figure came closer, gun in hand, and into the circle of lamplight. Not his dad. Surely he was hiding, too. Or looking for something to use as a weapon.

Mark wanted to ease the door shut, but knew that even the slightest movement might be seen. He froze, watching as the man approached and reached out to turn off the TV set. Silence dropped like a bomb. Mark's lungs were nearly bursting. Silently, slowly, he released the breath he was holding and drew in another. Through the narrow crack, he clearly saw the face of the intruder.

This could be helpful, he thought. If the man escaped, Mark could identify him later. He took careful note of the features as the man examined something on the shelves above the television, probably his dad's trophies or grandad's gold pocket watch mounted under a little glass dome. The man's back turned as he headed for the desk on the other side of the room. Then he whirled around quickly, alerted by car doors slamming outside. There were voices. The cavalry had arrived! Good for Dad!

The man cursed and disappeared from view. Mark remained where he was. The police were here and everything would be fine now. A bit of excitement, having a burglar. His mates had never had anything like this happen in their houses. He smiled with anticipation. Tom and Hugh would turn absolutely *green* when he told them about it.

He almost came out of the cabinet then so as not to miss a minute of the arrest, but remembered his father's orders. Mark had been working hard on his impulses since he'd turned thirteen last month. Self-control was imperative now that he was no longer a kid. His dad would be proud that he'd followed instructions to the letter. A good soldier, my lad, he would say. And one day Mark would be.

Doors slammed again and shouting commenced. Shots were fired! Crikey, he wished he could be out there to see the arrest. Maybe he would be asked to appear in court later to identify the chap who broke in.

His leg cramped horribly and his neck began to hurt, but he held steady. Dad would come soon.

"Where is the son?" a deep voice demanded. Mark peeked out of the crack in the door. Mr. Lazlo, who worked with his dad.

"No sign of anyone else here, sir," A uniformed policeman said. "Only the body in the kitchen."

Body? Mark burst out of the cabinet and scrambled to his feet. He dashed, arms flailing, legs half numbed, right past Lazlo and the copper. His socks slid on the tiles when he hit the kitchen and he tumbled forward to his knees. "Daddy!" he screamed, voice breaking, heart breaking.

Strong arms clasped him from behind, lifted him forcefully and pulled him away. "Come with me now, Mark. He's gone. You don't need to see—"

Mark stopped struggling and stood stock-still. He was no match for a grown man's strength. Not yet anyway, even though every vestige of boyhood drained out of him then and there. He took a deep breath, inhaling the metallic scent of his beloved father's lifeblood now puddled uselessly on the kitchen floor.

"I *do* need to see," he said, staring down at the body. "I'm going to kill the man who did this, Mr. Lazlo. On my honor, I swear before God, I will kill him," he muttered through his teeth.

Lazlo rested his hands on Mark's shoulders as they stood together. His voice was deathly quiet as he promised, "Come with me, Mark. I'll help you."

Chapter 1

Paris—Present Day

Mark felt pretty naked without his favorite sidearm, especially when everyone else he'd met was sporting fully automatics. He was seriously underdressed for the occasion.

"Sonny is making a few calls," the woman at his side told him. "If you check out, we can use you, Alexander. If not…well, let us say you need not worry about future employment," she added with a catlike smile.

His cover was solid thanks to Corbett Lazlo, Mark's mentor and employer. He understood why the woman didn't trust him. Hell, she had excellent reasons, better ones than she knew.

He had wormed his way into this nest of snakes with a few phone calls and by dropping the names of a couple of very recently deceased criminals who were probably well known to her and thought to still be alive. Identity theft in its highest form worked wonders, or so he hoped.

"Come along, darling. You might as well meet the rest of the merry band while we wait," the woman said, ushering him up the steps ahead of her. She wore unrelieved black. Probably matched the loaded accessory she carried in her pocket with her finger on its trigger.

This infiltration seemed the best method of discovering the whereabouts of the man who had murdered Mark's father sixteen years ago, an assassin called Trip. Mark's job, as well as his lifelong ambition, was to capture Trip and determine who had hired him. The killer's trail—an exhaustive list of murders stretching over almost two decades using the same MO—had led Mark to this woman's address.

Something about Deborah Martine seemed familiar to Mark. Not so much her looks as her mannerisms, the way she moved, a fleeting expression. Something. Martine was not her real name, he was sure. But none of that mattered at the moment. This fortyish, unnatural blonde with bedroom eyes, a commanding attitude and an evil sense of humor, was his ticket in. Sooner or later, she would lead him to Trip.

She could use more hands and another gun, she had told him when he introduced himself earlier that afternoon. Apparently she was also looking for someone adept at bypassing the newer security systems on the market. He couldn't believe his luck there. He assured her he'd been sent by a trusted mutual acquaintance. The woman was no fool. She had verified his identity. No problem. Lazlo had expected he would be checked out and had prepared for it.

At the top of the stairs, she reached past him, opened a door and entered, standing aside for him to follow. Mark glanced around the dimly lit room. They were in an office in the upstairs of a run-down warehouse south of Paris near the Seine. He could smell the river, feel its dampness, even inside the building. Two men were seated on the dusty chairs and a woman stood against the wall in the shadows.

She looked up as he approached the table. The dim glow of the lamp illuminated her face. Mark's heart nearly stopped. There was not merely something familiar about this woman. He *knew* her! Worse than that, *she* knew him. One word from her about their former connection and he'd be dead in the water. Literally. His body adding to the river's pollution.

He saw the flicker of apprehension in her eyes. And a question. Should she take him out? She was asking herself. She was armed and it wasn't apparent that he was. But for some reason, she didn't act.

He suddenly realized she was as vulnerable as he was. If she killed him, she would have to explain why. And if she declared who he was, the others would suspect her, too. *Takes one to know one*, he thought with an inner grimace.

Had she turned? Her looks had changed radically. Maybe her allegiance had, too. Or had she been a subversive even when he had known her during their training op in the States? She could be working undercover, of course. God, but he wanted to believe that. He had a soft spot for her, but he couldn't let that distort his reasoning or affect his decisions.

He could kill her, right now during her hesitation. He still had his knife, which he could bury in her throat before anyone blinked. But then *he* would have to deal with the fallout. If he used the hidden blade, he would be weaponless except for hands-on. That would be patently ineffective against bullets.

Even in the unlikely event that he managed to kill everyone in the room and survive, his ultimate goal would be impossible. Deborah Martine was his only lead to John Trip, the assassin he had spent over half his life tracking, the man he meant to destroy no matter the cost. He might never get this close again. No, he couldn't compromise that goal as long as there was the slightest chance to see it met.

And he had to acknowledge that the woman feigning nonchalance in the shadows might possibly be here for a legitimate reason, just as he was, and didn't really deserve to die.

He had a feeling that fate had another of those unfunny life-altering jokes in store for him, like the sudden gut-twisting attraction that had driven him crazy when he had known her before. She had damn near caused him to lose control and break his steadfast rule concerning personal involvement. Even so, he had little choice now but to let fate rule in this instance. He would have to allow Renee Leblanc to live and see what happened.

Renee leaned against the rat-infested wall, one booted foot propped on an old crate. In her right hand, she held an unlit French cigarette. Her left rested on the unsnapped holster of her nine millimeter.

The man who entered the weak circle of light thrown by the antique gas lantern registered a barely discernible flicker of surprise, just as she suppressed one of her own. *My God. It was Mark!* What the hell was *he* doing here? Her heart rate doubled and her breath caught in her throat. Instant recognition promised instant death if he blew her cover.

Her fingers slid around the grip of her H&K pistol, its coolness and texture her only comfort.

"This is Mark Alexander, everyone," Deborah Martine announced as she took a seat at the head of the scarred table.

He was actually using the name she had known him by. Not a good sign that he was undercover. But then, she was using hers, too, though it was necessary in her case.

Deborah inclined her head at Renee. "Meet Renee, our explosives expert."

Deborah's lazy gaze swept on to the slender, shifty-eyed thug on her right. "Piers, provisions." Then to the beefy Neanderthal at the far end of the table. "Etienne, muscle." She offered a secret smile before turning her attention to the rest of the group. "Mark will handle the security systems for us." Her left eyebrow rose as she addressed him. "That is, *if* your credentials are in order."

Renee's eyes again locked on the newcomer. Her first instinct had been to shoot him where he stood before he could say a word. *Protect the mission* was a mantra she lived by. Self-preservation was an even stronger motive. She figured he probably entertained similar thoughts of eliminating her as a threat, but had no weapon.

Either he had flipped at some time during the past two years, or he was working an op for SIS, the old MI-6. Problem was, she knew nothing about an ongoing operation in Paris involving the Brits. However, given the dearth of official information exchanged by intel agencies who worked for the *same* government, it was reasonable that she'd be in the dark about a foreign one. Why would the Brits inform the U.S. when infiltrating a terrorist cell in France?

Since Alexander hadn't yet opened his mouth, she would give him the benefit of the doubt. If he revealed who she was, he would expose himself.

Same with her. She raised a brow and offered him the ghost of a smile. He returned it, just a small quirk of his lips. Nice lips they were, too. She remembered them well. Their texture. Their taste. Their hunger that had fueled her own. A spike of warmth shot through her. Make that heat.

One kiss, mind-blowing as it had been, did not provide a basis for putting her life in the man's hands. That killer body of his could be just that, the body of a killer. The memory of how her wayward mind had wandered directly to him the morning after that kiss, as she hovered between sleep and wakefulness, disturbed her even now. She had clearly visualized him, standing in the shower, soaping himself, his head thrown back, exposing his strong, corded neck as if he invited her to put her mouth there and feel his quickening pulse. Her own body had hummed.

Renee shook her head. The vision firmly engraved on her mind might have been buried, but hadn't lost its clarity.

Renee straightened and pushed off the wall, taking a seat on one of the overturned boxes that served as extra chairs. "Where are the others?" she asked, ignoring Alexander as best she could.

"Checking the perimeter. Sonny and Beguin will be up in a few moments. Tonight's the night we get down to business," Deborah announced.

Finally. Renee kept her expression bland. She knew the job, in general anyway, and hoped to find out where the strike would occur so she could get people in place to prevent it. This was yet another planning session. Deborah seemed to get off on having rendezvous in secret locations, the seedier the better.

Sonny's last job had been an attempt to abduct a U.S. senator's son. It had been foiled by the Secret Service and Renee's team, COMPASS, one of the civilian special ops teams formed under Homeland Security. The giant, more commonly known as Sonnegut, had escaped capture and fled here to France, doing a bang-up job of covering his tracks.

But Renee had located him.

Her stated mission was to identify Sonnegut's affiliation, find out who was behind the kidnapping attempt and determine what they had been after. Indications were that the motive had been political. So far, she had tailed him until she could befriend one of his cohorts and work her way into this little gang.

It was a start. Deborah Martine was Sonnegut's lover. Renee had begun to suspect she might also be the person in charge. The question was whether or not she reported to someone else, higher up. Unfortunately Renee thought she might have to abandon her primary mission in order to throw a monkey wrench into the strike the cell was planning. But first she needed to discover how the group was financed, and, most important, the target and timing of their strike.

Renee had struck up an association with Martine,

gaining her trust in the guise of a French-Canadian expatriate whose father owned a demolitions business based in Calgary and who had taught his only child everything he knew about explosives, hoping she would carry on.

Her cover contained a great deal of truth, but there were no records available to prove or disprove it. She had told Deborah at the outset that her father had disowned her and she had intentionally "erased" herself. Martine had professed to admire her precautions and apparently accepted her story.

Demolition was a handy skill in the underworld, much in demand. Credentials weren't required. The proof was in the execution, so to speak.

Renee glanced again at Mark and saw that he was assessing her, no doubt wondering if she had switched loyalties. Neither of them had any option but to play this out, at least until they could talk in private. And even then, would either dare admit why they were really here? As far as he knew, she could be exactly what she appeared to be. And so could he.

Every tenet of her training demanded that she erase any threat to her mission. So would his. They had trained together in the life-or-death black ops field, after all.

Two years ago, the FBI had hosted an international working seminar on nontraditional methods of dealing with terrorists. Fifty elite agents from as many organizations had attended. No operative had been identified other than by name, no countries or organizations revealed.

At the time, Renee had figured Mark represented the U.K. because of his accent and surname. And that polite reserve of his had seemed distinctly British to her. Maybe her assumption had been wrong. Ordinarily she knew better than to assume anything, but it hadn't really mattered back then.

Even at first glance, just as it did now, her heart had raced with both fear and fascination. Aside from the wide shoulders set on a body that wouldn't quit and a face that boasted intriguing features, her attraction to him surpassed the physical. There was something dark about Alexander that went deeper than the fathomless eyes that seemed to peer right into the very soul of her. He made her feel exposed…vulnerable…hot. What's more, he made her like it. Dangerous, indeed.

When she'd known him then, just as now, she had needed her entire focus to remain on the job. Renee had staunchly kept her distance. But she'd sensed a definite reciprocal interest, proved beyond doubt when he had impulsively acted on it. And kissed her. Afterward, they had avoided each other and only spoken in passing when paired off in a shooting match.

Even so, she'd hardly been able to concentrate whenever he was in the vicinity. And the vision of him naked that she hadn't consciously sought, yet couldn't seem to dismiss hadn't helped. Renee had

vowed early on that until her career was well established and she had proved her worth, a personal life
would be out of the question. Apparently Mark's
goal hadn't been any different.

Avoidance had become a game until their schooling was over and they parted company with merely
a couple of satisfied nods, wordlessly acknowledg-
ing their shared battle and mutual success.

In retrospect, maybe she shouldn't have been so
hell-bent to deny any interaction. At least then she
might be able to guess something about his mind-
set now.

Sonnegut slammed into the room, his great
height and boisterous energy almost comical considering the secretive nature of the meeting. He was
a good-looking fellow of German extraction, cocky
as hell, larger than life, auburn-haired, blue-eyed,
built like a monster truck. There was simply too
much of him to be believed.

Beguin followed him, a pale shadow in
Sonnegut's wake. Thin, dirty blond hair hung like
fringe over his craggy features. Darting close-set
eyes peered from behind the sparse strands. He
moved like a wraith and always gave Renee the
creeps. She prided herself on her uncanny recognition of accents, but she hadn't figured yet where
Beguin had hatched. He never had a word to say.

Deborah Martine's eyes lit up and a smile curved
her generous lips whenever Sonnegut appeared.
"Everything as it should be, Sonny?" she asked,

her voice rife with authority. Her attitude had become increasingly bossy lately, Renee had noticed.

The big man nodded and shot her a merry grin. "I had to get rid of a vagrant. He was getting too curious."

Martine's smile slipped at that. She probably worried about the eventual discovery of an errant body mucking up this new meeting place, but she said nothing more about it. "I meant the phone calls you were to make regarding Alexander. Results?"

Sonnegut brushed his hands together and nodded vigorously. "He's solid. Brugel said he does good work, so did Hamish. Best they know of for providing surreptitious entry. Both vouched."

Martine reached inside her pocket and retrieved a cell phone that must have been set on vibrate. She clicked it on, listened, nodded and answered briefly and affirmatively in Italian. It was the third language Renee had heard her speak fluently.

They all conversed in French, of course, except when Martine encouraged her to use English. That was Martine's native tongue, though she was as proficient in French as anyone born to it. Apparently she was pretty good in Italian as well. She was speaking with the man called Brugel, whom Sonnegut had just mentioned.

After she put the phone away, Martine promptly handed over a nine-millimeter pistol to Mark. "Here's your toy back, darling. You're hired. Same rate as Brugel gave you, agreed?"

He nodded, pulled a wry face as if disappointed

that he wasn't offered more and stuck the weapon beneath his black leather jacket. His intense gaze captured Renee's again. His dark eyes told her nothing regarding his true affiliation. But they did reveal his continued interest in her as a woman. Not helpful at all.

Then Deborah turned to Renee. "Tonight we firm up some of the details. Also, if you have any doubt about your ability to do what we need done, you must tell me now. Failure is not an option."

Renee shrugged one shoulder and tried to look nonchalant. "I can handle anything but boredom," she declared lazily, leaning backward as Mark pulled a lighter from his pocket and offered to light the cigarette she held.

She lowered her lashes, then raised them in shameless flirtation. Had to keep up the act. "Thank you for the thought, but I don't smoke anymore. This," she said, wiggling the cigarette between her fingers playfully, "reassures me of my ability to resist temptation."

He raised one dark brow, his expression deadpan as he drawled. "*All* temptation?"

Renee smiled, trying for coy. She caressed his well-honed body with a slumberous appraisal, fully aware of everyone's eyes now riveted on them. "Well, only what I have sworn off of as not being *good* for me."

Deborah cleared her throat. "Not to interfere with your charming little tête-à-tête, my dears, but I believe I have the floor. And we are on a tight schedule with this lovely conference room."

The men, except for Mark, laughed at Martine's sarcasm, nudging one another playfully like naughty little boys. Their deadlier forms of naughtiness, especially Sonnegut's, made her sick. The memory of the bullet-riddled bodies of two Secret Service agents reared its ugly head.

She could wind up exactly like them if she put a foot wrong. That was another reason she never allowed personal relationships to develop. The more people you worried about leaving behind, the less effective you were when faced with a deadly situation. And loved ones could be at constant risk just by association.

Renee carefully concealed her thoughts and smiled along with the thugs. "Please, continue," she said to Deborah with another casual lift of her shoulder.

Martine looked from one to the other of the group, then concentrated her full attention on Renee. "You have examined the blueprints I gave you?"

"I have."

"Good. I will identify the target now."

She pulled a wrinkled map from her coat pocket. "Here. It is marked and the address is written along the margin. It is to be totally demolished, as if clearing the area for future construction. Spare all surrounding structures. The destruction must be isolated."

"Implosion." Renee took the folded map and

tucked it inside her jacket. "So you want the adjacent buildings undamaged. Why?"

"It is to be very clear what our target was when it is finished." Her smile grew hard. "That's enough information. Yours is not to question why."

"Ah, mine is but to do or die," Renee said lightly. "I got it." She squinted at Deborah. "How critical is it that the target collapse directly into its own footprint? It could take months and a very large crew to give you any sort of guarantee on that. And even then…"

The woman huffed and rolled her eyes. "Just do the best you can with the time you have, girl. You said you were the expert. And if you need a crew—" she gestured around the table "—here they are."

"The hour's late," Sonnegut said with an impatient gesture. "I have other things to do. Could we get on with this?" He shot Deborah a heated look that indicated these things had little to do with the business at hand.

"Of course, darling. You're right as usual." Deborah gifted Sonnegut with a salacious look.

Renee listened as Martine instructed the others in their respective tasks, each of which was to assist Renee in her assignment in a particular way. Apparently Mark was to circumvent any security systems and get them inside the building to wire it.

"You will be notified of the next meeting," Deborah said, indicating the meeting was over. She glanced at the newcomer. "Take Mark in hand, will you, Renee?"

Renee bit back a protest. "I suppose he will provide good cover during our planning foray. We can be lovers discovering Paris in the cold November rain. What do you think of that, Mark?" she asked, drawing out his name suggestively.

"I'll try to be of more use than the cigarette," he replied with a sardonic smile before getting up to follow the others out of the room.

Renee was the last to leave and Deborah stopped her at the door. "A word before you go." She leaned out onto the landing. "Sonny, give Mark his instructions, won't you? Tell him what to watch for? I'll be along in a moment." Apparently satisfied by the answering nod, she closed the door on the men.

"Now then, Renee, you have everything you need?"

"For now. I'll give you a list of the matériel I require once I have it?" Renee said. "Do you think you'll have any problems acquiring it? Dynamite's easy enough, but RDX might prove difficult."

Deborah patted her shoulder, an almost motherly gesture. "Send me a complete list. The supplies will be available when we are ready to put things in place. Anything you require. I'll have the elevations delivered to you as soon as I have them so that you and Mark can study the exterior."

She held up a finger, shaking it like a schoolteacher admonishing a pupil. "Keep a close eye on Alexander," she ordered, then added with a leer, "I'm sure you know exactly how to insure his loyalty. He is well vetted, but we both know how tenuous a man's fealty can be, don't we?"

Renee laughed, injecting a scoff. "I've had more experience learning *that* than I have time to tell you. Any man can be bought, but you and I know the currency they favor most, eh?"

"I sensed you were savvy in that regard. You remind me of me," Deborah said with a satisfied bob of her head. "Let me know immediately if you have any problem with him and I'll find you a replacement."

Renee promised and said good-night, knowing full well what Sonnegut had been instructing Mark to do while Deborah gave her orders. He would be set to watch her even as she watched him. That was probably another of the reasons he had been hired.

The irony of their keeping tabs on each other struck her as funny, especially if Mark *was* still an operative for his government.

However, if he had turned she might just die laughing.

Chapter 2

Once they had left the building, Renee turned to Mark. "Do you know anything about demolition?"

"Do you?" he countered, one dark eyebrow raised.

"Do you have a place to stay?" she asked, ignoring his question.

"No, I only arrived this afternoon." He walked beside her, hands tucked in his pockets against the bitter cold, obviously willing to follow wherever she led.

"I have rooms in the Latin Quarter. You'll stay with me."

Better to keep him close, as Deborah had ordered, and find out what he was all about than to wonder where the hell he was and what he was up to. She didn't expect to get much sleep, if any, in either case.

"Are you giving me a choice?"

"Sure." Renee headed for her rental car, a puke-green Peugeot with a balky transmission. "You could go back and bunk with Deborah and Sonny. How do you feel about threesomes?"

He laughed, a brief, bitter sound. "I don't see *that* happening."

"Who are you working for?" She hoped to catch him off guard with the question, but he replied immediately.

"You, of course."

Right. Very smooth answer and quick on the trigger. He wasn't going to tell her a damn thing. And she wasn't about to volunteer anything until she knew which side he was on.

If he was working undercover, as she was, his suspicions would mirror hers. If he had flipped since she knew him in the States, he might try to kill her. Alert to that possibility, she kept enough distance between them to respond to any attack he made. She was pretty sure he wouldn't do anything until he knew for sure what she was really doing here.

They got in the car and she drove like a maniac on the streets of Paris. Like everyone else did. When she came to a screeching halt on the curb in front of her apartment building, she noted his knuckles were white as he loosened his grip on the dash. He exhaled as if he'd been holding his breath.

"Here we are. I'll go up first. Give me a quarter hour alone, then come up to 304. Knock twice, then once."

"Got it," he said agreeably. "What's with the code?"

"Old habits die hard," she replied.

"So do old operatives in case you plan to wait behind the door to do me in."

"If I planned to kill you, I would have done it already."

He quirked an eyebrow. "I thought the drive here was an admirable first attempt. Nearly caused my heart to fail."

"You have a heart? You're in the wrong line of work." Renee got out, slammed her door and left him sitting in the car, hoping someone would steal the wreck tonight so she could legitimately request another.

She could picture Mark on his phone the second she disappeared inside, either checking with his control on her current work status or calling Deborah Martine to reveal who she was and asking how he should dispose of the body. By the time he did either, she planned to know more about him than his own mother did and act accordingly.

The instant the door closed to her room, she was hitting her speed dial. "Get me whatever you have on British operative Mark Alexander. All sources. Instantly. It's crucial. If you can't find him in SIS, check other agencies, home and abroad. Then go to

private. Also run him as a skel. He could be dirty."
She clicked off.

Renee felt extremely isolated on this op. Minimal
phone contact, documents left at a specified drop
and no face-to-face with the other agents in place.
Three of her fellow COMPASS agents were here in
Paris, waiting to help her wrap this up when the time
came. Until then, she wasn't supposed to reach out.

And the role she had assumed for the op—cocky,
expatriated Goth chick and experienced killer with
no conscience or morals—was wearing thin. There
was no break from the act. She wished she could
talk to someone as herself, just for a minute or two.
She missed speaking English, though her French
was fluent. She had acquired it as a child right here
in Paris and fine-tuned it under her mother's
tutelage. Her knowledge of demolition had begun
then, too, as she and her mom followed her dad
from job to job. No one knew more about the
business of leveling a landscape than Ed Leblanc.
And she was trading on his name and reputation.
Though retired in Miami for several years now, a
bogus Web site, created specifically for this assignment, had him listed as still running a world class
business out of Calgary, Canada.

She missed her mom and dad, her friends and her
apartment. Renee let her thoughts drift to her home
in McLean, Virginia, where Christmas decorations
would be going up in stores even though it wasn't
quite Thanksgiving. Holly would be feeding her

fish, tending her plants and collecting her mail. Unless Holly had been called away on assignment. If so, someone else would hold down the fort, one of her fellow agents. They provided good support on the homefront. But this was her first international assignment. It required a great deal of improvisation and all the acting skill she possessed. And she wasn't used to going it alone.

Now she had a partner, of sorts. That just went to show, one should be careful what one wished for. Company could be deadly. As a fellow operative, Mark would judge her without mercy. And if he turned out to be a traitorous sonofabitch, he'd probably wind up trying to kill her, again without mercy.

Suddenly isolation seemed the lesser of two evils, but one she couldn't afford.

Anxiously she waited for the report on him. "C'mon, c'mon, I don't have all *night*," she grumbled, frowning down at her cell phone.

Mark cursed as he put his phone away. Not a thing on her. Nothing! Lazlo had pulled every string available within the short amount of time he had with no results. None of the agencies, government or private, in the States or Canada, had a listing for Renee. He had captured a photo of her profile with his phone as she drove through the city at breakneck speed. She wasn't in any database Lazlo could access which left damn few.

Corbett Lazlo could accomplish virtually anything, connected as he was. He had survived a conviction of treason, escaped prison and proved himself innocent. After that, he had refused to return to MI-6 where he had worked with Mark's father and had begun his own company. Lazlo operated without the confines of bureaucracy that hobbled the government organizations. And ignored most of the rules. He was a law unto himself. Mark admired him more than anyone he knew. If Lazlo couldn't get a background on this woman, then it couldn't be had.

So who the hell was she? He knew she had been cleared to take that course at Langley. If she had been dropped by one of the agencies since then, there would be a record of it somewhere. That meant she must be working at a job important and secretive enough to have her background totally erased in case someone went looking. This was a good sign actually, he realized. If she were a traitor, even a suspected one, the word would be out on her.

He didn't have to wonder what she would manage to uncover about *his* past. It wouldn't look good. His real background had been replaced with one so unsavory it scared even him. She'd be horrified that she'd ever gotten close enough for that kiss they had shared.

Odd, the compulsion he was feeling to spill everything to her, to assure her he wasn't the lowlife his official records stated. Maybe he had a death wish hidden somewhere in his psyche. More likely his libido was fogging his brain. God only knew how he had resisted involvement with her two years ago. The feelings she engendered then were suddenly active again.

That lovely smile of hers combined with all that barely suppressed energy had gripped him fiercely the minute he'd set eyes on her at the initial training session. Instant accord between them, and she had felt it, too. He had nearly lost his grip on reality and offered her more than he could afford to give. Thank God, he had come to his senses in time. Still, he wouldn't take anything in exchange for that one long, soul-deep kiss.

The girl was a chameleon, but looked great in both guises. Before when he had known her, she'd seemed the wholesome, suntanned, athletic type, maybe a girl who had a couple of brothers to toughen her up a little and make her competitive. The way she looked now, she could be belting out hard rock on stage or hanging out on street corners peddling S&M. Scary as hell, but wretchedly enticing for all that. It made him wonder which was the real Renee Leblanc.

It wasn't entirely her looks that fascinated him, but more the way she carried herself, handled herself and met every challenge. She woke something in him that had lain dormant all his adult life. Not that he wasn't interested in women, just that he had never before craved anything more than a very temporary hookup.

He wanted her. There was also this odd, almost compelling urge to befriend her. He couldn't thank her for that. Hell, he didn't make friends. He didn't need them. But there was something about her that he knew he couldn't leave alone. Not this time.

She had this bit of vulnerability that he figured no one saw but him, hidden as it was in those whiskey-colored eyes that would make a man as drunk as the real stuff if he drank too deeply.

Her hair had been longer and silky two years ago. Now it was chopped in a chin-length spiky hairdo he found rather silly. What man would want to run his hands through gelled spikes? Still, even that anomaly flattered her features.

Yes, she was a beauty, especially with the added fire of her attitude. Alert, interested and therefore wildly interesting. He couldn't ignore that heavenly body, toned to slender perfection. He remembered her in the gym, slick with sweat and wearing only a sports bra and shorts. The memory threatened to activate his own sweat glands.

He had to exercise strict discipline and keep this under control. He was older now, more committed than ever to the mission he had sworn to complete and no woman was going to get in his way. Not even this one who affected him more than any other ever had. The fact that she had that effect made him slightly angry with her. Or perhaps with himself.

Mark climbed the stairs and gave the knock as she'd instructed, fully aware that she might try to kill him the instant he entered the room. It would be interesting to see which of them had benefited most by their Langley training. He was fairly sure he could take her, but not absolutely certain of it. That only added to the mystique.

She opened the door and stepped aside, gesturing him to come in. "You're a real piece of work, Alexander. Have been for a very long time. Must have made a distinct impression on Sonny when he made those calls. Sit down," she said, indicating the two chairs placed near the room's one window. She remained standing. "Why was your name deleted from the course records? There is no mention of your training, training I *know* you had."

"What training would that be?" He glanced meaningfully at the window, reminding her that anyone with a parabolic microphone could be listening to every word.

"Don't worry, this place has been screened to hell and back, as well as those buildings across the street. No ears. No cameras. I'm very thorough."

"And quite mysterious," he commented. "Apparently you don't even exist other than in my feverish imagination."

Her full lips quirked at his sarcasm. "Feverish? Why, Mark, I'm so flattered."

He smiled back. "No birth, no schooling, no employment, not even a driving license." He recalled the ride here. "But that last bit I can well understand."

"You might have found something under my maiden name had you bothered to ask what it is."

Mark was already shaking his head. "You weren't married, either. Not officially anyway."

She strolled to the window and raked back the sheer curtain to look down at the street below. "What's your real agenda here?"

He stood and headed for the door. "Food, bath, sleep, in that order."

She dropped the curtain and headed his way. "There's a café several doors down that's open late. Food's cheap but edible."

He was a bit surprised at how easily she acquiesced but held the door for her to exit first. "So long as we won't need to *drive* there."

They took the stairs at a fast clip, Mark preceding her as she insisted.

He found himself actually looking forward to spending time with Renee, an unusual turn for him to take when he knew very well he ought to be working this alone. He always worked alone. He didn't like having to worry about anyone else's safety. Or their potential for making mistakes.

She would only get in his way, distract him, maybe even get one or both of them killed if Trip was around and in his usual form.

He thought about how ironic it was that the very lack of available information about their previous occupations in intel had virtually verified their loyalties.

What a strange world it had become. At any rate,

Mark felt like celebrating the fact that he didn't have to kill her.

They exited the building and she turned left. Mark walked beside her, confident they had a sort of truce going on.

"If the wine proves drinkable, perhaps we could have a little toast," he suggested. "Something along the lines of good health and long life."

"Or world peace," she said with an inelegant snort that made him laugh.

"Ah, but then we'd both be out of work, love."

She stopped, halting him with a hand on his arm. "Did you cross over, Alexander?"

"Did you, Leblanc?"

For a long moment, she stared into his eyes, then threw her trust at him like a fast ball. "No, I didn't. I'm working."

He almost groaned. Was she mad? She must be to grant him that much information without even knowing him. "So I suppose this is where I declare undying love for my country and promise to fight evil to the death?"

She inclined her head and pursed her lips. "Yeah, Mark, this is the place where you do that. Only you had better make me believe you."

"Or you'll do what?"

She smiled and managed to look downright evil. "Or I will kill you. Right where you stand."

It was only then that Mark felt the gun barrel prod his belly.

Chapter 3

"Deborah, you try to make me jealous? Is this why you hired Alexander? I do not trust him in spite of the glowing recommendations."

"Do not try my patience, Sonny," she warned. She watched him study her face and knew he wondered who she really was. If he knew, he would be more afraid than he already was. Cassandra DuMont held more power in her small, soft hands than this man could ever imagine. She toyed with the idea of telling him, but decided against it.

Sonnegut was a tool. The double entendre of a thought made her smile as she stroked his sweaty brow. She raked a beautifully manicured nail along his cheek, scraping the roughness of stubble that had caused a delicious burn moments earlier. In bed, he was unequaled, even by John Trip. Trip's value lay in his inventiveness. Sonny's size and boundless energy provided an interesting contrast.

He kissed her gently. "You are such a soft, cultured creature, Deborah. Not at all like the women I am used to."

"Soft?" She laughed at that. "Only on the surface, darling."

He sighed and lay back, one hand behind his head, the other toying with her breast. "Ah, yes, there are times when I glimpse the steel beneath your charms."

At the moment, lying with him on silk sheets in her fancy rococo bed, she *was* soft and wearing nothing but a contented feline smile.

He exhausted her, helped her to sleep soundly, a feat for which she had amply rewarded him. This walk on the wild side had worked in that respect. She loved the edginess of it, operating in disguise, meeting in dark places, the risks of leaving behind the protection of who and what she was.

Becoming Deborah Martine allowed her a certain freedom and keen excitement that she lacked as Cassandra DuMont, doting mother to her son and the chief executive of her family business. Also, this little vacation afforded a perfect opportunity for another, even deadlier strike against Corbett Lazlo. She would give him his own mini version of nine-eleven and bury his people beneath tons of steel and stone.

Sonnegut stroked her tousled hair and inhaled the rich, heady scent of her perfume. He brushed the smooth curve of her lips with his, tickling them with his tongue. "Tell me that you are not attracted to this man, Alexander. You cannot trust him, you know."

She tweaked his chin. "Ah, darling, I trust no one."

"Not even me?" he demanded with a pretense of anger.

Cass rolled her eyes playfully. "Don't be tiresome, please!"

He rolled away from her and sat up on the edge of the bed. "First you enlist that...girl. She is dangerous, that one. And much too young to be of any use." Cass knew Sonny mistrusted youth. He probably recalled how he had misspent his own doing stupid things that had earned him time behind bars.

Cass sat up and trailed her nails down the center of his back. "We shall soon see what she can do. Alexander will keep an eye on her. As long as she does what's required of her, that's all that matters. Once we've accomplished our little task here in Paris, we'll no longer need either of them."

"Then I can kill them?" he asked, cracking his knuckles, obviously anticipating how he would do it.

Again she laughed, leaned her head against his shoulder and snaked her arm around his waist. "You are such a bloodthirsty savage."

"You like me the way I am," he said, reeking with confidence and manly sweat.

"At times like this, I admit I do," she assured him. Actually there were only two reasons a woman like her, with her upper-class education and manners, would have use for a man of Sonnegut's talents. He had just fulfilled one—messy, uninhibited sex. The other, he so far had failed. She would give him one chance to redeem himself. If not, then Trip would take care of him along with the others.

He got up and found the bottle of expensive Scotch they had abandoned earlier. Taking a slug directly from it and exhaling noisily, he looked down at her. "This plan of yours is too complex. Why not let me go directly to this man you want destroyed? Simple is better."

"You will do as I tell you."

"I will kill him for you. That will be the end of it." He took another drink and handed her the bottle.

"But I don't want it ended. Not just yet," she insisted. She raised the bottle to her lips, daintily sipped the Scotch, then rested the bottle on the bed beside her, cradling its neck. "I've only just begun to punish him. He deserves to suffer, to lose everything he has built for himself and everyone who is faithful to him. And he *will* suffer."

"I could bring him to you, let you inflict what you wish."

"As you brought the senator's son here?" she said angrily, taunting him with his failure. "That was supposed to draw Lazlo out and make him available for a strike!"

Then she relented, placating her lover. "I know, I know. That was not your fault, darling. How could we have known of the boy's interest in the president's daughter and that the Secret Service had him under surveillance? That was a fluke. If they had not already been in place and mucked it up, you would have been successful and the senator would have called in his old friend, Lazlo, to find his son. At least you got away and left no trail."

She sighed heavily and leaned back against the pillows, stretching out her arms to welcome him back into bed. "Come, let me show you how happy I am about that."

"Again?" he asked with a proud smirk. He lowered himself onto her body and she allowed him the momentary feeling of domination.

Yes, she would sleep well tonight. And she would dream of Corbett Lazlo's absolute destruction.

"Turn around slowly," Renee ordered. She slid her finger to the outer curve of the trigger guard, afraid to touch the hair trigger on her borrowed weapon. Mark couldn't see her do it since his back was now to her. It wouldn't do to kill him accidentally.

She walked him for several blocks, ordered him down a deserted side street and backed him to the edge of an alleyway. "Turn around so I can see your face." She needed to be sure. The streetlights were marginally dimmed by the fog and there were no lighted storefronts, but she could see.

As she looked into his eyes, she saw his gaze fly to one side and his features freeze. *What?*

Before she knew it, he had her pistol in his hand and turned on her. "Now walk calmly forward until we reach your little café," he ordered. "Then we'll have our conversation."

Furious that he had disarmed her so casually, Renee stamped on his foot. He didn't flinch.

"Temper, temper," he warned, grasping her upper arm in his free hand and duck marching her along the narrow sidewalk. "Is there a café at all or did you intend to leave me lying in the gutter, a poor homeless corpse?"

"Go left up ahead there," she gasped, belatedly wondering how she had lucked out and not gotten shot. What a stupid thing to do, reacting to the oldest trick in the book. *Look behind you.* She felt like an idiot.

When they entered the café, she realized he was no longer holding her at gunpoint. In fact, with his arm around her and her hand clutching the back of his, they must give the appearance of a couple unable to keep their hands off each other. He released her when they reached a table near the window and sat down across from her.

"What do you recommend?" he asked politely.

Renee took a few seconds to calm her breathing and gather her thoughts. "Coq au vin's good here."

"Too late for that, I expect. What of the cheese omelette?"

She nodded, noting the waiter already approaching the table. She remained silent while Mark ordered for them. She had noticed earlier that his French was perfect, not a trace of an English accent.

When they were alone again, he touched her knee under the table. "Here's your weapon. Safety's on."

"Thank you," she huffed, taking it from him while trying not to touch his hand. "That was *so* rude."

For the first time, he grinned at her and his face transformed. "Please, accept my apology. And I'll accept yours while I'm at it."

"Dream on."

The boyish expression and twinkle in his eyes fascinated her as did the lock of dark hair falling across his brow. She would never have guessed he had a devil-may-care side to him. It only enhanced the attraction she felt in spite of herself. And made her madder than hell.

"Disarming you was necessary to establish my sincerity," he told her. "A confession under duress is difficult to credit."

She acknowledged the truth of that with a brief incline of her head. Now, at least, she could believe what he told her. If he told her anything at all.

His expression grew serious and he seemed to arrive at some decision, even as she watched. "You could have killed me and you didn't, so I suppose I must trust you."

"I suppose you must," she said, holding a wide-eyed nonexpression. "So? What are you doing here?"

The pause lasted a full two minutes. "I'm trying to locate a man called John Trip. Have you heard that name since you became involved with this lot?"

Renee shook her head. "Nope, never heard of him. Why are you after him?"

"Why are *you* here?"

Renee sighed. "Sonnegut tried to abduct a senator's son in Virginia. We prevented that, but he got away. My job is to find out who ordered the abduction and why, then take them down."

"On whose behalf?"

"My government's."

"American, not Canadian."

"Yes. And you?"

When he neglected to answer, she prodded him. "Come on. Information is power here. Are you working for SIS?"

He shook his head. "A private organization that deals with threats, mainly against dignitaries, celebrities, politicians and the like."

She gave a single nod. "Must be Lazlo."

From his fleeting expression of surprise, she knew she had scored a direct hit with the first round, but he didn't admit it. He simply pursed his lips and narrowed those sexy eyes at her. Lord, there was that fluttery feeling in her stomach again. She tried to ignore it.

"The Lazlo group's not exactly low profile any longer," she informed him. "At least not within the intel community. They've lost a number of operatives lately. It's no secret someone's out to wreck the organization. We've been aware of it for some time."

"We?"

She simply smiled. She had the feeling he didn't engage in much conversation, even for his line of work. He struck her as a loner. A shadow.

The food arrived, so by tacit agreement they postponed the discussion. After they'd been served and the waiter had disappeared, eating became the priority as each retreated into private thoughts.

Renee's were bouncing around like crazy, her personal interest all tangled up with professional. Not good, she quickly realized and went about separating her intense curiosity from her critical need to know.

And to think, she had been ready to plead for this assignment if it hadn't been given to her. Her dearth of experience had been against her. Her youth, too, since she had just turned twenty-five. Only the facts that she could recognize Sonnegut and that she was the one who had determined his present location had put her at the head of the line. She was not about to let an inconvenient attraction interfere with her mission or cloud her judgment.

When they finished eating, Mark watched Renee plunk down enough Euros to cover the meal and the tip. He didn't object. To be honest, he wasn't certain of the proper etiquette. He expected to pay when he was out with a woman and always insisted, but this was no date. "The next meal's on me," he said.

He got up in time to pull back her chair and help her into the jacket she had slung over the back of it. She gave him a long-suffering look that poked fun at his manners and reaffirmed this definitely was no date.

She walked ahead and opened the door for him when they left the café, daring him with those whiskey-colored eyes to object. He didn't. He walked right past her with a nod of thanks.

They strolled side by side down the deserted street, hands in their pockets. Neither spoke until they had both made sure they weren't followed or watched. On some level, Mark enjoyed the shared duty. On another, he felt wary of it. She must be green as new grass or she'd be a lot more careful. Now he'd have to be responsible for her and that infuriated him. Precisely why he preferred solitary assignments.

"All right, let's have an understanding," she said in that take-charge voice of hers. "I have a job to do. You have a job to do. I don't like sharing any better than you do, but it's *need to know* time. If we don't lay all our cards on the table, we could each jeopardize what the other is doing."

"So deal."

"I did," she declared. "I admitted I'm undercover, you know why I'm here and that I'm not really working for these people."

"And I've told you that I'm after John Trip." He sighed and cocked his head to one side, waiting for her to continue.

"As I said, I'm following up on a political kidnapping attempt that resulted in the death of U.S. Secret Service agents. Sonnegut was there. I traced him here, discovered who he was working with and arranged to meet Deborah Martine."

"Why not Sonnegut directly?"

"Because I want to know as much about the man as I can and he isn't likely to admit things about himself that his lover might."

That made perfect sense to Mark. "Have you learned anything helpful?"

"Sonnegut's gang of four is apparently for hire, the men you met tonight. Now Deborah either hired them for this particular job, or Sonnegut hooked up with her and she's appointed herself captain."

"For what it's worth, I think she's the one running him," Mark told her honestly. It felt strange, collaborating. He worked alone. Lazlo usually just provided him with information or specific orders.

He watched Renee process the opinion he had offered. "Probably, but Sonnegut steps up and takes over just often enough to make me question that. If Martine is the boss, she's letting him think *he* has more power than he actually does for some reason. She is the one who offered me work."

"Setting explosives."

Renee nodded. "That was my ticket in. We met over a bomb, so to speak, and I think that incident inspired the idea of using explosives. I don't yet know why she wants to blow that building, but I'm working on it. Now who is this Trip guy you're after and how does he figure into this?" she asked, reverting to his mission.

"He killed someone, years ago. A man who meant a great deal to me. And to Corbett Lazlo," he added reluctantly, granting her more trust than he was comfortable with.

Mark had had to relinquish his former investigation into the threats against Lazlo and the recent assassinations of a number of Lazlo's agents. Others would continue that probe in earnest, of course. Lazlo knew finding Trip was Mark's primary goal in life.

"So it's personal?" She leaned toward him a little, revealing her eagerness. That she would let him see that gave Mark a bit of reassurance.

"A vendetta, you mean? No, it's business. He's already murdered at least two Lazlo operatives in addition to the man I mentioned. He might be responsible for others that we don't yet know about if he employed other methods. But we're certain of these three. He left proof. Trip's a paid assassin."

"Which means that someone hired him to do the killing. You need that name," she guessed correctly.

"Obviously. How close are you to finding out what you need to know?"

"Not close enough. Sonnegut runs the boys and Deborah runs him. But who they report to, if there is a higher authority, is anyone's guess at this point. So far none of them has provided any hint of motive. But even given Sonnegut's attempted kidnapping of a senator's son, I sense this current operation is not political and certainly not ideological. It has to do with either greed or revenge."

Mark wondered how good her instincts were and whether he could rely on them. As a hard and fast rule, he relied on no one but himself. And Lazlo, when necessary.

The last time he had actually known anyone well enough to trust them, other than Lazlo, was when he was thirteen. He had relied on and trusted his dad, above all. And there had been Tom and Hugh, his best friends, his trusty mates since early childhood. He still kept up with their lives because he cared about them, though for their safety, he'd had no actual contact with them since his disappearance the night of his father's death.

Trust and reliance he granted only to true friends, not chance acquaintances like this woman. And at present, he realized, he had no real friendships. None whatsoever.

She went on, oblivious to his thoughts that excluded her. "Sonnegut doesn't seem enthusiastic about any of it. It's almost as if he's along for the ride. But Deborah gets this crafty look. Did you notice?"

"She can't wait to see it happen," he agreed, nodding. "Seems a bit psychotic if you want my opinion." He wasn't used to giving out his thoughts, but she was damned easy to talk to. She smiled in response.

"I wish I had more time to find out what's behind

this, but I can't very well plan the implosion of a building while I'm filling in the gaps. If this is to go down soon, my people will have to take whoever I've been able to identify and just hope somebody will sing." She grinned at him then and bumped him playfully with her elbow. "You Brits say that, too? Or do your perps *peach* on each other?"

"Sing, squeal, rat out. Yes, we have that in common." And very little else, he reminded himself. Renee defined the term extrovert and he might as well wear a recluse sign around his neck. Colloquialisms would probably prove the least of their differences.

He had mastered what he could of American slang, but his time in the States had been brief, he had always disliked American films and television, and he'd never had the opportunity to make any Yankee friends.

Again he thought, no friends at all. Corbett Lazlo was the closest thing to it, but even their interaction was based on a mutual goal. And technically, Corbett was his boss.

He admitted there were disadvantages to working completely alone, but he reminded himself sternly that he still preferred it. Even during his required military service he had remained a loner. It was difficult for him, sharing information, but necessary in this instance. Renee was right about that. He would have to make the effort.

Mark ran a hand through his hair and rested it on the back of his neck for a minute. "Martine is my only lead to Trip. Depending on how quickly this job goes, there might not be enough time."

"Deborah's not likely to tell *you* anything about John Trip," Renee said, "and he's obviously not one of the gang. Maybe I could help. What if I told her that I'm looking for someone to do a little wet work to cover my tracks on another job?"

Mark was already shaking his head. "Not feasible unless you're wallowing in wealth, in which case you wouldn't need to be doing what you're doing."

"Ah, so this Trip is outstanding in his field, huh?"

"One of the best. A legend in his own time. Charges a fortune."

"What's his connection to Deborah? I wonder…"

Mark held the door for her as they reached the apartment building. "If I knew that, I wouldn't need to be doing what *I'm* doing." He paused in the doorway, frowning down at her. The dim lighting threw shadows across her features and he could see nothing soft in them. "I have to locate this man, Renee. You'll have to find a way to stall the demolition until then."

"How close are you?" she asked, starting up the stairs ahead of him.

He tried not to notice the sway of her hips right in front of him. She wasn't trying to be provocative, but his eyes were not cooperating with his brain. He wrenched his thoughts back to the subject at hand.

"Until a week ago, Trip was in Liverpool. He disappeared before I could get him, but I found a discarded cell phone with his prints on it. It was crushed, but I managed to retrieve phone records. Five calls were to Deborah Martine here in Paris. There were two incoming from her."

"Aha, sounds like a real relationship," Renee quipped. "So you're pretty sure he's here in Paris?"

"Possibly. If not, I mean to find out where he's gone."

"I'll help you," Renee offered, "if you'll help *me*. Try to find out who Sonny answers to." She smiled up at him. "And if I can manage to get chummy enough, I'll ask ol' Debbie if she's got a squeeze ol' Sonny's not wise to."

A *squeeze*. He liked the term. Rather crass and usually reserved for females, but probably descriptive of the power-mad Martine's lovers.

He thought about squeezing Renee and couldn't seem to dismiss the idea. *Main squeeze* stuck in his brain like a song fragment that played over and over.

Why was she so open with him, so trusting? What sort of agent took chances such as that? He admired her courage but wondered about her sanity.

But then, who was he to judge? He was well aware that he had not had the usual experiences of someone who'd led a regular life. Since the age of thirteen, and probably even before that, he had been trained not to trust.

But he had trusted Renee tonight more than he had anyone else in a very long time. She had that effect. Alarm bells were ringing in his head. This woman was dangerous on so many levels.

Renee watched as Mark opened the door to her apartment and entered first, his weapon in his hand.

She resented that. It was her place to clear her own quarters. He would bully her if she allowed it, but she decided to choose her battles. If she didn't, they'd be at each other's throats the entire time.

He rejoined her in the small sitting room. "Looks okay."

"Thanks. Excuse me for a minute." Renee immediately went into the bathroom, turned on the water and made a phone call to see if there were any further results to her earlier inquiry. Nothing had changed, but she hadn't really expected it to and was glad it hadn't.

She believed Mark. He'd never have gotten into the course they had attended together without a bona fide and rather remarkable association with one of the elite forces battling terrorism. Lazlo had an excellent rep. They hired the best and got results.

"Where do I sleep?" he asked when she returned.

She pointed to the antique recamier, a one-armed lounge that wasn't even comfortable for sitting, much less sleeping. "I'll get you a pillow and a blanket."

He sat on it, bounced once and frowned. "And perhaps a back brace for the morning?"

Renee turned away from him as she suppressed a laugh at his expense.

He had a dry sense of humor, but his having one at all surprised her. He almost never smiled without qualifying it with a lift of that left eyebrow. "For a homeless person, you're not very appreciative."

"I was hoping you might want to keep me under closer surveillance for the night, in the event I'm not really who I say I am."

"Share my bed?" She chuckled. "And here I thought Brits had no sense of humor. You're a riot."

He grinned. "And I was under the impression Americans were…unreserved."

"Profiling at its worst, I guess. I'll get you that pillow."

Renee left the room in a hurry, hoping he hadn't noticed that split second of consideration she'd given his suggestion.

They were unwilling partners now and would be pretending an intimate relationship during the coming days. The idea of establishing a real closeness with him to insure his help and full cooperation was so unprofessional it was laughable. And tempting, she had to admit.

Really, really tempting.

Chapter 4

Sleep had proved elusive at first with her guest in the next room stirring restlessly as he tried to get comfortable. But eventually Renee slept for exactly four hours and woke refreshed. Her internal clock operated without fail, always had.

Her skill at remote viewing had been amazingly productive this morning, too, she thought with satisfaction. Good to know *that* wasn't going to suffer because of the distraction sleeping on her sofa. She had worried it might, since Mark had virtually waylaid her subconscious that morning long ago when she visualized him taking a shower. Her particular and unusual ability had secured her the job with the team of agents who had talents similar to

hers and she would hate for anything—or anyone—
to interfere with it.

She loved what she did. Usually. In any case, the
remote viewing she did was not exactly hardship
duty. She liked putting it to good use and it didn't
sap her energy, give her headaches or other bad
effects. Unless she counted the uncomfortable
feelings of arousal the vision of Mark had caused
her back in the training course. No more of those,
she promised herself.

Immediately on waking, she always focused her
mind on Deborah Martine. This morning the
woman appeared to be in her apartment. Or town
house. The exact location or layout was never clear,
but it was definitely Deborah's abode.

Renee had "been there" before, a number of
times, in different rooms. Three images presented
this morning, an unusual occurrence: Deborah,
Sonnegut and another man, one Renee had never
viewed before. This was the only person outside the
current group that Deborah had met with, at least
in the early morning.

Renee sat up and grabbed her sketchbook, quickly
recording the details she had gleaned before they
escaped her. The visions came easily most of the
time and played out like disjointed videos without
sound. Some were clear as day. Some were hazy,
nearly indistinct and colorless, a bit like half-remem-
bered dreams. This morning's had proved exception-
ally good. She wielded her pencil with confidence.

Architectural details of the building's exterior came first. She needed to locate the building and these new image fragments would surely help. Double arches, done in stone. Old and in need of sandblasting. Hmm. Not that unique in the older section of the city, but that in itself was a clue. At least it narrowed the search area. When she exhausted those particular clues, she turned to the new face on the block, the interesting stranger.

Tall, almost as tall as Sonnegut. Dark, handsome, deadly. She wondered if this man could be the one Mark was seeking. Pencil flying, Renee laid down the gesture drawing that would serve as a guide for a more detailed delineation of features.

Trying hard to recapture every nuance of the vision, she closed her eyes again, seeking clearer memory of her impressions.

"So you lied."

Renee jumped, her pencil and pad flying out of her hands as she dived for her weapon.

A large hand clamped around her arm. She checked her response, which would have broken at least his thumb, maybe his wrist. "What are you doing in here?" she demanded.

"Better question. Why did you lie about having seen Trip?"

"I *didn't* see him until just now!" she exclaimed, realizing too late what an explanation of that would entail. And how unlikely it would be that he'd believe it. Still, there was no way around it unless she lied again.

He released her, crossed his arms over his chest and glared at her through narrowed eyes. "Just now," he repeated, glancing around her messy bedroom. "Hiding in your wardrobe, I suppose?"

Renee shook her head and grimaced, seeking a way to begin that wouldn't make her sound certifiably nuts. She inhaled deeply and began to explain. "Do you remember the studies undertaken in the seventies? The ones that explored the…inexplicable? Project STAR?"

"Psychic phenomena," he said, tongue in cheek. "Discontinued after your military intel community computed how little bang they were getting for the enormous number of bucks they were shoving down a rat hole?"

Renee took another deep breath and tried again. "No, it's ongoing. They turned it over to…another agency that had fewer constraints and better funding." She added a smile. "I was…*am* one of their subjects."

He brushed a hand over his lower face and shook his head. "You're telling me that you're psychic."

"Not precisely. I'm an RV."

"Ah. A recreational vehicle. This gets better and better. Makes me want to kick your bloody tires."

Renee laughed. "No, a remote viewer. I…see things. Places. People."

He waved a hand at the sketchbook lying on the floor. "John Trip."

"That's really him? I thought it might be. He's at Deborah's apartment this morning."

"Really. You've been wafting through the ether. What a convenient trick that must be."

She closed her eyes for a second. "Look, I know this must be hard for you to believe, but…"

"I want an address," he stated. "A real address where I can find him, Leblanc. And cut the bull."

Renee bit her lip and got up off the edge of the bed. She was getting a crick in her neck from looking up at him. Also, she didn't want to feel as open to attack when she answered. "Look, I'm sorry, I can't give you the address. Not yet anyway. I don't know where she lives."

Again he grasped her arm, his fingers like a vise. "So meditate a little if that's what it takes and *get* one."

"Doesn't work that way," she admitted, frowning at her arm. "You want to let me go before you leave bruises. I warn you I don't react well to pain."

He let her go with a little shove. "I had almost begun to trust you, damn it. If we're on the same side, why won't you help me?" He flung a hand toward the sketchbook. "You obviously know him. Tell me where he is."

She clasped the front of her nightgown, blousing it a little so she wouldn't feel quite so exposed. He had been glaring at her breasts until she reacted, then he forced his eyes away from her. A muscle ticked in his jaw.

She relaxed a little. "I can't and I am sorry. You'll have to help *me*. I need to search for the building where Deborah's staying."

Renee picked up the sketchbook and turned the page back. "See this? It's the first time I've gotten anything on the exterior of her place. It could belong to a quarter of the buildings in Paris, but at least this cuts down my search."

He stared at the drawing and then at her. "You actually think I'm buying this fairy tale?"

Renee shrugged. "Suit yourself. It's the best I can do. I work better with a clear and rested mind so mornings are optimal. Soon as I wake up, I give it the old college try. This morning was pretty successful." She tossed the sketchbook to one side. "But all I'm likely to get today."

His laugh sounded bitter. "My God, you're a nutter. Who are you really?"

"Exactly who I told you I am. I work for a special unit under the auspices of Homeland Security. I used to be with the Secret Service. Our current team consists of agents who have, well, special abilities."

"Hallucinations, apparently."

She cleared her throat. "In a collaborative effort, we managed to find Sonnegut. We determined he was in Paris, then located him in a popular café. After that, I simply went there, followed him in person and later managed to meet with Deborah Martine."

"But you've never been to her home?"

Renee shook her head, meeting his eyes, trying to convince him that she wasn't fabricating all this. "She's very secretive about some things. At least, with me she is. Obviously Sonny and this Trip guy know where she lives. They're there. Or at least they were about half an hour ago."

"You're bloody serious!" he said, his gaze penetrating as a laser beam. Then it softened to sympathetic. "You actually believe you *see* these things."

Renee smiled and shrugged her shoulder. "How else could I have gotten a likeness of your Mr. Trip?"

His jaw slid to one side as he regarded her, now with a sardonic expression. "Because you've seen him before. In the flesh. Where, Renee?" he demanded, softly this time.

"Only in my *mind*. I'm being straight with you, Mark. I've never seen this individual in person, I swear. If I knew him and knew where he was, I would tell you. I have no reason to lie about it. He's nothing to me unless he was the one calling the shots on the kidnap plot I'm investigating, or maybe this planned bombing. And from your description of him as an infamous paid assassin, I don't believe that's the case."

His gaze glanced off her chest again and settled on the window. "To hell with this. I'm going for breakfast."

"I'll come with you. Wait a minute. I can be ready in two shakes." She seriously craved coffee.

Much to her surprise, he was waiting for her in the other room when she emerged dressed in her leather miniskirt and a jacket that covered her holstered weapon. She ran her fingers through her hair and fluffed it, deciding to do without the dark lipstick, pale makeup and black eyeliner she usually wore.

He was dressed in the same well-worn black jeans, pullover and jacket that he'd had on the night before. Other than another eight hours' worth of whiskers, he looked much the same as he had last night. Disreputable, sexy, dangerous.

"I still don't believe you," he muttered as they took the stairs down to the street.

"And I don't care," she replied. "I'm not here to convert you. If you want my help, I'll give it. If not, take a hike." She scooted around him and took the lead out the door, not caring in the least whether he followed or went in the opposite direction.

He followed all right. "I'm not letting you out of my sight. You know Trip."

"Yeah, well, we could play *do not, do too* till hell freezes over, but I'd rather table this until after I get some coffee in my system. You'll get the guy. Just be patient."

"Why don't you have coffee and food in your flat as any normal person would?" he demanded.

She shot him a killing look. "Because obviously, I'm not *normal!*"

Breakfast was a silent affair. Croissants, orange marmalade and coffee went down like ambrosia, calming nerves and stimulating thoughts.

After a while, the silence grew too loud. "I don't cook," she added for good measure.

He licked marmalade off his thumb, then looked a little embarrassed that she caught him doing that. "So," he began in an obvious attempt at conciliation, "were you born with this...ability? The remote viewing thing?"

Okay, maybe he was trying. She would, too. "Pretty much. Had it since I can first remember things. Used to scare me when I found out I was weird like that. Now I understand it better. Sometimes it still throws me for a loop. It's not always accurate and almost never dependable enough that I can call it up at will."

"Convenient," he said with a pursing of lips. "I've never met anyone who claimed psychic ability before."

"Officially I sort of fall under the psychic umbrella, but probably not in the sense you mean. I can't mind read or predict the future or tell you where to find grandma's long lost ring. Nothing like that. All I can do is see where I'm not. Not *everywhere* I'm not. Just certain places. And even then I don't always know where those places are."

"I'm surprised you admit limits."

"There'll be a person, someone we in the business term an *outbounder*. In this case, I'm using Deborah. I can sometimes home in on where she is and often see her surroundings, who she's with and so forth. Sort of like through her eyes, or at least as if I'm right beside her."

"Wow," Mark said with an attitude of blatantly fake admiration. "That is so amazing."

Renee laughed, signaled the waiter and pointed to her cup. "You are such a snot."

"Pardon?"

"Pardon, hell. You heard me. Lighten up, Mark. I'm not trying to hoodwink you or anything. Believe me or not, I told you I don't care. You're not essential to my plans." She lowered her voice and leaned toward him as if imparting confidential info. "But I might very well be essential to yours! So you'd better be nice to me."

Mark let the matter drop. The woman was crazy and there would be no reasoning with someone as delusional as she was. Maybe his best bet was to humor her, pretend to believe she could do what she thought she could. She believed it. He was pretty well convinced of that.

He had heard of remote viewing, of course. He'd also heard of fairies and leprechauns. The anger he felt wasn't directed at Renee. He actually felt sorry for her. His fury was for those who had encouraged her to believe all that rubbish.

Her government and his had sponsored all sorts of trials, trying to verify and incorporate paranormal powers into intelligence work. As far as he knew, it had come to nothing and only wasted a great deal of time and money.

And yet, he had read something about the Japanese.... No, it was all wild fantasy. If anyone had ever succeeded in proving the existence of such powers—and either establishing that proof or disproving the claims altogether should be a relatively simple process—it would have been all over the news.

Wouldn't it? Or would it be kept under wraps and used? The thought gave him pause. No, he still didn't believe her.

They took the Paris metro to Courbevoie, in the Northwest suburbs, and spent the day canvassing the location around the building in which she was to plant the explosives.

When they first arrived at the location, Mark had hidden his surprise. He hadn't noted the address earlier. Lazlo owned this property. It was one of three locations Mark knew of in Paris. One was an older building in the heart of the city. The other was the new super office building that had been completed last year. It was located nearby in the heart of the ultramodern business section of the city, La Défense. This one was the former headquarters building now used for private consultations with clients who needed anonymity for their association with Lazlo, Inc. Some of the offices on the middle and ground floors were leased to other private companies. Mark understood there was still a tech-rich command post in the basement beneath this building that employed a number of Lazlo's specialists, though he had never entered this building himself.

Very few knew what this building housed. The Parisian operatives who worked there and the clients themselves would, of necessity, keep the location private. The secrecy of its identity could prove a valuable clue to why this building had been tagged for destruction. Why not the newer one that was now the center of Lazlo's organization? Perhaps it wasn't yet known to the perpetrator? If destruction of Lazlo property was the only objective, why not the older structure that would be infinitely easier to access than this one?

Since he and Lazlo were certain that two of the Lazlo operatives had been murdered by Trip, it stood to reason that more were being targeted here in Paris, probably with this bombing. It was all connected, Mark realized.

This was a departure from Trip's MO, at least that they were aware of. Maybe he had killed in other ways before, perhaps even in this way, without claiming credit. He could be in charge of the entire plan.

While Renee scouted the building, he made a quick call to Corbett's private number and advised him about the bombing and John Trip's probable involvement.

The conversation was brief and to the point. Lazlo wasted no time making a decision. "Business as usual will continue there so as not to alert them. They might go after another location and give no warning at all. Play along. Just make certain the building's never actually wired. Make your position solid and get all the info you can before you take Trip down. Is that understood, Mark?"

"Affirmative. Have you had any more e-mails?"

Mark asked. There had been numerous threatening messages, their source untraceable.

"None in the last week. Perhaps our fellow is busy making plans to carry out his threats," Lazlo said with a note of bitterness. "No luck tracking the origin of the messages as yet, but Lucia's giving it all she's got. It's only a matter of time. She's the best."

Lucia. There was a certain note in Corbett's voice whenever he said her name. Corbett would mention an operative here and there as if Mark should know them personally. But he didn't, of course. He didn't even know them in passing. He was not a company man, but Lazlo's private hire, a solitary weapon. His time was spent on the road, never in an office, and his only contact was with Corbett himself.

"So, what is your function in this?" Lazlo asked.

"I'm to bypass your security," Mark explained. "I'll have to give them something believable."

Lazlo issued a chuckle. "Go ahead and show off."

Renee was returning. "I'll call when I have news," Mark told him and rang off.

He decided he wouldn't mention the Lazlo connection to Renee. Her mental stability was definitely in question at the moment. He sighed. But he certainly couldn't fault her appearance. Saucy, sexy as hell and infinitely pleased with herself as she strode toward him smiling.

If she knew the reasons behind the choice of targets, she hadn't revealed that to him, but he truly believed she had no clue. Neither did he for certain.

But it didn't take a genius to deduce that this planned attack had everything to do with the recent attempts to decimate Lazlo's organization.

He accompanied Renee when she went inside on the pretext of finding a particular office. All the floors were inaccessible past the lobby's black marble desk. While Renee chatted up the male receptionist, saying she was lost and looking for some business office or other, Mark surreptitiously eyed the surveillance cameras and bank of elevators outfitted with sophisticated scanners. Lazlo wasn't joking. Security was tight. But not impenetrable.

"How peculiar is that?" Renee asked after they left the building. "There are no public offices. They don't even have a sign. What is that place anyway?"

"You heard the spiel. It's a private company that takes its privacy and that of its clients very seriously."

"One of the great mysteries of life, I guess. Well, we're finished reconnoitering for today. Let's get something to eat. I'm starved. There's a place."

She pointed to one of the cafeterias, Paris's original answer to fast food long before they embraced golden arches. Strictly tourist fare.

"Fine," he said, though appalled at her choice. He would have preferred a burger and chips if she was operating on a limited budget or possessed no taste buds.

"Not exactly haute cuisine, is it?" she commented as she chose an entrée that looked very much like lumpy mud. "That's not too bad. I had it once," she informed him, pointing at something resembling chicken parts swimming in oil.

"Once was probably enough," he mumbled, but went with her suggestion since nothing else looked more palatable.

After they were seated and opening the small bottles of wine they had purchased for the meal, she stopped what she was doing. "Why are you being so sulky? You've hardly spoken to me all day."

"Didn't want to interrupt any *voices* you might be hearing from the beyond," he said, poking at the chicken on his tray.

To his surprise, she laughed and went on with her meal, such as it was. He toyed with his, hating every bite. Finally he gave up. "Why are we eating this tripe? Anyone who comes to Paris and settles for this should have—"

"Her head examined?" Renee said, finishing his sentence. "Well, I just wanted to see how far you would go in humoring me. Do you really think I'm totally barmy? Isn't that the word you Brits use? Barmy?"

"A bit outdated, but yes, that would be appropriate enough," he agreed with a succinct nod.

"Thank you, Dr. Alexander." She smiled and shook her head, then polished off her wine. "Ready to go? I need to report to Deborah and see if I can get her to meet with us in person. Maybe she'll invite us to her place. Once we locate it, you can set up surveillance, maybe see Trip if he comes back. I need to put someone there, too, to keep an eye on things. I'm worried about the explosives she's able to get."

Mark watched her closely. "So you didn't sense that Trip was staying there with her?"

Renee shook her head and looked pensive. "Nope. They have more than a business relationship going, I think, but no. I got the feeling they were solidifying a deal or something. Handshaking and so forth. Sonnegut was there. Maybe Trip's involved with the bombing. Or could be they simply happened by her place at the same time. Must have been a little awkward for her if that was the case and the visit was personal."

Mark nodded, encouraging her to go on. "So you didn't get any…audio?"

"No, doesn't work that way. I get glimpses of what she's seeing, occasionally a glimmer of feeling, that's all. No specific thoughts, no words."

"Ah, I see."

"No, you don't *see*. You still don't believe a word of it," she said casually as she pushed away from the table and stood. "But that's all right."

Mark took her arm, walking beside her as if they were a couple strolling together, anticipating a leisurely evening in Paris. It was freezing outside, but he ignored the chill. It was no greater than the one inside him.

He had really thought for a little while, even secretly hoped, that they would be working together for real, trusting, helping each other with their respective missions. The feeling had proved unique, the lack of aloneness, the anticipation of sharing something.

Now he knew he merely had an added responsibility. Protecting her from her delusions.

Chapter 5

On the way back to her apartment, Mark reached for her hand and laced his fingers through hers. All for the pretense, of course, in case they were being watched. She didn't appear to object. In fact she smiled up at him, making him feel as awkward as he had the first time he'd ever held hands with a girl. And how long ago had *that* been?

Mark remembered attending a birthday party once just before becoming a teenager. The sister of one of his mates at school had a well-chaperoned dance celebrating her turning fourteen. He and Hugh had been coerced into partnering two of her younger friends.

Strange he should recall that today of all days. Part of the entertainment had been a fortune teller.

The old woman the parents had hired, decked out in her wild gypsy finery, had delighted in reading their palms. Until she had come to Mark. She had seriously scared the stuffing out of him with her words. "I see great tragedy. Much blood. Hide when it comes. You are a seeker. Know when to cease probing or you shall die."

"We *all* die, madame," he had said, faking a belly laugh for the sake of the others listening to the dire projection.

And yet, the blood iced in his veins as she spoke her final warning in a deep rasping voice. "Never mock what you do not understand."

He was doing that now, he realized. Though the old gypsy's dire prediction had come to pass in less than three months, Mark had never associated his father's murder with that foretelling. He didn't now, really, though in retrospect it did seem strange.

That had definitely been a tragedy with much, much blood. And he had hidden. And he had been seeking the killer ever since. First, in preparation for the task with the help of Lazlo and the training he'd provided. Later, in earnest, as he followed every snippet of information that might possibly lead him to John Trip. He might well die if he succeeded in finding the murderous bastard, but he was taking Trip down with him.

"I apologize for mocking you," he said to Renee. He couldn't take her remote viewing fantasy seriously any more than he had accepted the warning of the old gypsy, but he should stop ridiculing her. He doubted she could help herself. No doubt, she'd been brainwashed by those who tested her. His protective instincts had kicked in with a force that surprised him.

She grinned at him and squeezed his hand. *"There are more things in heaven and earth, Horatio, than are dreamt of in your philosophy."*

He laughed. "Ah, so now you're seeing the ghost of Hamlet's father?"

"Nah. I don't believe in ghosts."

"But you do believe you can see things that aren't there."

"But they *are* there," she insisted. "They just aren't necessarily where I am at the time."

"They are where your, uh, outlander happens to be?"

"Out*bounder*," she said, correcting him.

"And you could select anyone you choose for this role?" he asked, fascinated in spite of himself. She was so specific about it, even though she had admitted the visions themselves were fallible.

"Anyone I've met and made some sort of connection with." She ducked her head then, watching her feet as they walked over the uneven cobblestones. "Actually I have to like them a little to do it. That's one of the drawbacks I'm trying to work with that's the most troubling. Given my job, the most helpful outbounder generally would be a criminal of some kind."

"And you *like* Deborah Martine?"

Renee shrugged. "I had to work really hard to find something about her that was admirable enough to latch on to."

"And that would be?"

"She loves her family. Her father, who is dead now. She admitted how hard she's worked all her life to make him proud of her. How much she admired him and wanted to follow in his footsteps."

"Who was he, Hitler?"

Renee laughed. "Owned some sort of business. She wouldn't go into detail about it. She has a son, too. Though she worries about his rebellious nature, she said he would one day accomplish all the things she was never able to do as a woman."

"So the lad's slated to blow up the world? She actually told you about her family?"

"And she asked all about mine. Of course, I manufactured most of what I told her, but she responded with a few little stories of her own. I sensed hidden issues, but she seems fiercely loyal, at least when it comes to blood ties."

Mark snorted. "You find her *admirable?*"

"Not in the general sense. Deborah's a determined criminal if not a terrorist. But that one particular human aspect of how she loves her family gave me a way to connect with her. Fortunately that proved enough."

"Which could very well be fabricated, just as

yours was," Mark pointed out. "I can't see her loyal or loving to anyone."

Renee shrugged. "Maybe not, but leave me that much so I can keep connecting with her, will you? It was damned difficult and took a while before I could manage even that."

"So you can choose who you do this with? Could you do it with me, for instance?" When she shot him a weary grimace, he persisted. "If you found something to admire about me, that is? Why not use me tomorrow instead of Deborah?"

"What good would that do? Just leave it alone, Mark. I would never have told you about it anyway if you hadn't seen the picture I drew of Trip."

Mark decided not to pursue that for the moment.

It bothered him that she found anything to admire about Deborah Martine. He had a very strong aversion to the woman and had felt it the moment they first met. She was a snide, cruel, oversexed bitch with a homicidal streak. That was how he viewed her. And if Renee possessed any sort of soft spot for the woman, it could prove fatal. "Surely you don't trust her, even a little," he said, a last attempt to get a handle on the erstwhile friendship.

"Trust Deborah? Now who's barmy?"

Mark guessed he might qualify. For some odd reason, he had begun entertaining the idea of testing Renee. Not that he had one ounce of faith in what she claimed to be able to do. Still, Japan had that ongoing program they felt was working. And if Renee wasn't lying, so did the U.S.

"I think you should consider giving me proof of what you say you can do. Use me. Let me go somewhere and you can tell me where I went. Then I'd believe you."

"I don't have time for games," she said firmly and proceeded to ignore him. Except for the hand that seemed restless within his. He caressed her palm with his thumb, their fingers still laced together.

She broke their physical connection immediately and stuck her hand in the pocket of her jacket. "I mean it, Mark. I *really* don't have time for games."

The package of elevations arrived by courier soon after they returned to Renee's apartment. Deborah had vetoed a face-to-face meeting. The unsigned instructions ordered Renee to mark the insertion points for the explosives and indicate the amounts to be used and the peripheral equipment required for the implosion.

They spent the evening examining the detailed architectural drawings of the actual structure, floor by floor. Renee had the blueprints, too, and had been working on those long before she'd been given the actual address.

"You obviously know what you're doing," Mark commented as he watched her work. He admired her concentration and dedication to detail. And the endearing little crease between her eyebrows that came and went as she perused the plans. He found it difficult to keep his mind on his own notes regarding the security.

She stopped, pencil tapping rhythmically as she looked up at him. "Anyone can blow things up. It takes expertise to implode a structure. This usually takes weeks, sometimes months and requires several experts to confer on it. But as you heard her say, my time will be short so I'll have to do the best I can. It has to be done right. I can't afford to fake it."

"You've done this before…legitimately?"

"I know how in theory and have helped set up several similar events, but even experts consider this dicey. They plan, check, recheck and check again. My dad had the best crew ever. They never made a mistake. See, there is no school for this. Demolition people just breed more little demolition people. The only way to learn it is by interning with the best."

"That's how you got this assignment," he guessed.

"Not really, no. That was because I located Sonnegut," she said, tapping her forefinger on the plans. "Unless I've got her figured wrong, Deborah will have someone go over this, someone in the know. And she'll probably have a guy lined up to see that I set everything correctly. What if that's Trip? Has he ever used explosives to kill?"

Mark couldn't be sure. "Not that we're aware of. Three shots to the head is his usual. And he leaves a calling card. Wants full credit for it."

She rolled her shoulders, stretched for a minute

and started back to work. Mark went out for food, saw that she ate it, then made her stop when she looked too exhausted to work any longer.

"Good night," he said when she was about to close the door to her bedroom. "I'm going out in the morning. You're supposed to keep an eye on me, remember? Deborah's orders."

"Will you give it up?" She laughed a little and shook her head as she closed the door between them.

He stayed awake half the night studying what she had done and marveled at the amount of planning involved in arranging a building's implosion. Fascinating business. She must be a genius in math and physical engineering. What the hell was she doing working as a government agent, putting her life on the line this way?

Finally he finished his own notes and went to bed, choosing to sleep on the carpeted floor instead of the stupid fainting couch that was a foot too short for him and packed tight with horsehair.

When morning came, he had a plan to carry out. Her curiosity would get the better of her when she woke up and found him gone. She would have to check on where he went and would either follow him physically or try to locate him with her so-called psychic gift.

The fact that he half believed she had one disturbed him. He wanted her to be normal, damn it, not some bloody seer he could never hope to understand.

* * *

Renee groaned when the sunlight fell across her face and woke her. Her head ached and her neck felt as if someone had starched it. She stretched, rolling her head to one side and then the other, eyes still firmly shut against the unwelcome rays.

Three arches appeared, gray, the middle one yawning as doors within it opened. Pigeons flew, their flapping wings causing a momentary disruption of the view. Sidewalk art, very well done, the Mona Lisa. Feet walking on the face. The vision faded, sort of panned. Scaffolding. Buttresses.

"What in the world are you doing *there?*" she muttered to herself. In another part of her mind, she realized this vision loomed remarkably clear, much more solid than it would be as seen through Deborah's eyes.

Mark. She knew without checking that he was not in the apartment. "Why, you devil," she grumbled. He had put the suggestion in her mind last night, damn his hide!

She deliberately erased thoughts of him and tried to zone in on Deborah. No luck. His interference annoyed her, though she understood what Mark was trying to do. No, what he *was* doing. But he had cost her an opportunity.

Sighing, wishing she had coffee, Renee took a quick bath and dressed. Her plans were almost finished and Deborah wanted those and the list of further supplies within the next couple of days.

Though Renee felt secure in providing the correct placement, maybe she should consult by phone with her father, who indeed had run an international demolition company until his retirement. But on further consideration, she decided to rely on her own expertise and not involve her dad. Detonation was the tricky part and that would never take place anyway since this was just a setup.

This op had to be played out to the millisecond. Everyone involved must be taken down at the last minute and to the last individual. The building would never be at risk because she wouldn't be using anything that would actually detonate. But unless the whole crew was rounded up, someone would be coming after her.

They were a pretty tight-knit group, bonded by the expectation of exorbitant amounts of money. Renee's outrageous demand when she'd signed on hadn't even raised an eyebrow. Sonnegut and Deborah had okayed it without a blink. She wondered if Deborah had secured the loyalty of *all* the men in the same way she had suggested Renee secure Mark's. The more Renee considered it, the more she agreed with Mark that Deborah was the boss, but she still had no answers to the questions that had brought her here.

Renee sat at the table and worked a while, glancing up as Mark entered. "Hi. I hope you brought sustenance?"

He held up a huge cup of coffee and a bag from

the local patisserie. "Get your sketchbook," he ordered as he set the food on the table next to her.

"I'm busy," she argued. "This has to be done when the courier comes for it."

Mark ignored that, opened the bag of breakfast goodies, then looked around for her pad. He laid it on top of the blueprints and placed a pencil on top. "Draw where I was this morning."

Renee smiled. "Ah, the doubting outbounder. What makes you think I like you enough to use you? Maybe I didn't *care* where you were."

"Show me," he demanded. "If you want me to believe you, draw where I was and what I saw."

She picked up the cup, leaned back in her chair and cradled the coffee with both hands, bringing it to her lips for a sip. She couldn't resist annoying him since he had dashed her chance to locate Deborah's place of residence. He slid his jaw to one side and raised an eyebrow, daring her to prove herself. She smiled and shook her head. "I really don't have time to satisfy your curiosity."

"I insist." His mobile lips drew into a firm line and his dark gypsy eyes narrowed. "Do it. Or can't you?"

Renee tired of the game. "It would take too long to draw Notre Dame, Mark." She wiggled her fingers in the air. "All that fancy stonework and perching gargoyles."

His mouth went slack and his eyes widened as he stared at her. Then he blinked and frowned. "You...you followed me."

Renee rolled her eyes and plopped down the cup.

He moved the sketchbook away and stared down at the blueprints. "You've done more on these. How did you do all that and follow me?" His voice had dropped to a near whisper, as if he were speaking to himself.

Renee knew it was time to get this over with so he would leave her alone to work. Maybe leave her alone forever if it scared him enough. That would be best for both of them. Things were getting a little too tense between them not to end in another kiss. Or more.

"Okay, you went to Notre Dame. Saw a sidewalk artist's rendition of Mona Lisa and disturbed some pigeons. You walked around to the side, at least far enough to see the buttresses clearly. Oh, and the doors opened for people to enter as you watched. But you didn't join them."

"And then?" he demanded. "What did I do then?"

She sighed and crossed her arms over her chest. "I assume you went for the coffee and pastries after that. I tuned out and went to work. I have better things to do than sightsee vicariously. Now if you're through with the third degree, I need to get back to business."

He stepped back and turned away as he ran a hand through his hair. Now he believed her. There would be more questions, she was sure, but he was busy right now being gobsmacked, as the Brits so colorfully put it. Served him right.

For good measure, she picked up the pencil,

quickly doodled a little gargoyle, the one he'd been looking at last, on the margin of the building plans.

Mark suddenly turned back to her and frowned, then the gargoyle on the blueprint caught his attention. After staring at it for a long moment, he headed for the door. He opened it and went out without a word.

Leave it to her to rock a guy's world. What would he do now?

Chapter 6

Mark walked for hours, up toward Sacré Coeur, through Montmartre, giving only cursory attention to his direction. He had to come to grips with what had happened. It was true, all of it.

Renee had not followed him. She had been sound asleep when he left. That little kittenish sound she made wasn't one she would fake if she wanted to feign sleep. He was certain there wasn't a woman alive who would admit, even to herself, that she snored.

The Mona Lisa picture was what clenched it for him. No way could she have seen that, even if she had physically followed and looked on from a distance. It was flat on the ground and Renee had not been anywhere near the plaza in front of the cathedral. No, she had been right there in the apartment. Only she had somehow seen Notre Dame right along with him.

He hadn't missed her drawing of that gargoyle, either, the very one he had concentrated on, simply because it reminded him so much of one of his old professors, Sharp Beak, as they had called him. Even if she'd been there in the plaza and watching him, there was no way she could have known which figure he noted unless she had seen it through his eyes.

Damn. This was too strange. If he believed all this, then he had to credit that she *had* seen John Trip. The man was in Paris and cavorting one way or another with Deborah Martine. He was somehow involved in the plot to blow up Lazlo's building.

Mark stopped and looked around, suddenly realizing he didn't quite know where he was. Nothing looked familiar. This was one of the older streets. The building facades butted right against the narrow sidewalks.

Half columns bumped out of one, oddly shaped and imposing. Unique. Those he *did* recognize. He had seen them before. Somehow, some way, something had led him to the place Renee had sketched yesterday morning. Or perhaps he had passed this way years ago and some trick of subconscious memory had led him back again.

Mark crossed the street and ducked inside the recessed doorway of the building across the way.

Yes, it looked very much like what she had drawn. He noted the number on the door and walked down the street. Etched into the second story corner of the building, he saw the street name. *Rue de Courcelles.*

This, like Renee's apparent talent for remote viewing, was entirely too inexplicable for comfort. Nevertheless, he waited and watched for several hours, but no one came or went from the building.

Eventually he gave up and walked until he found the nearest metro station. This might all be a dream. He might wake up and find he had never gone to Notre Dame at all. Maybe he had never even made it to Paris or met Renee.

Hell, at this point, he was ready to question his own existence. She had damn well better have some answers when he got back.

"All right, I've found your building," he announced as he entered the apartment.

She reclined on the recamier, posed like a sinuous feline, the image compounded by the way she was licking a scoop of lemon ice affixed to a small sugar cone. He had seen the vendor pushing his little cart along the street outside.

His pulse increased as he took in what she wore—a skinny strapped black leotard that needed no bra. And she was barefoot, wiggling her toes as she noticed him noticing.

He couldn't help smiling. "Take your pleasure where you find it, eh?"

She saluted him with the cone and grinned. "It pays to stop and taste the ice cream. So what building did you find?"

"Martine's."

"What?" She looked delighted. And delightful, he had to admit.

"I'm not certain she has the whole building. It's not all that large, but it could be cut up into flats and I have no idea which would be hers if that's so. But the facade matches what you drew."

"So how did you find it?" She sat forward now, eager to hear, her lemon ice ignored for the moment, dripping slowly over her thumb.

"I'm not altogether sure." Mark shrugged off his jacket, tossed it on a chair and removed his weapon, laying it on the side table near the door. "We need to talk about that."

She frowned down at her sticky thumb, then raised it to her lips. Mark followed every subtle move she made with fascination. God, she was so…deliciously uninhibited.

"Maybe you should accept it as serendipity and let it go at that," she said.

Serendipity, huh? He stretched down the tail of his shirt, took the chair across from her and sat, crossing an ankle over his knee. He hoped she wouldn't notice the state of his body, caused by simply watching her agile little tongue.

This wouldn't do. He shook off the buzz of lust as best he could and got back to business. "You know it seems far too coincidental, our little reunion taking place while we're on totally unrelated missions."

"It's a good bet they're not unrelated," she suggested, punctuating her words with a swirl of her pink tongue against the pale lemon sweet. Mark's heart rate bumped up another notch. At this rate, he'd need a pacemaker. Soon.

Again he tried to ignore the distraction. "And our being thrown together. Martine's doing, I realize, but why the two of us? We're both new. Why would she pair us with each other instead of with two of the trustees?"

Renee crossed her legs Indian style and crunched down on her cone. She chewed for a moment before answering. "She trusts *me*. Well, as much as she trusts anyone, I expect."

"She can't have known you long. How did you manage that?"

"Saved her life. A setup, of course. She and Sonnegut were in this dive. Apparently Deborah likes slumming with the riffraff now and again. Well, *someone* planted a crude explosive device beneath their Mercedes. I stopped her coming out of the club and warned her to call the police, get the bomb squad to defuse it." Renee laughed. "Well, she couldn't draw attention to herself by doing that, now could she? And none of their bodyguards would touch the thing."

He smiled. "Let me guess. You volunteered your services."

She smiled back and polished off her lemon ice with a crunch and a nod.

"Brilliant. How did you convince her you didn't plant it yourself?"

"Digital photos. I'm an amateur photographer, don't you know. Caught the guy in the act. She'd never seen him before and never will again, of course. I explained in minute detail what the bomb would have done to the car, not to mention herself. She was impressed as hell."

"Hired you on the spot, huh? I'm impressed, too."

"We met a few times over drinks so she could thank me properly. Once I revealed my background, she offered me work if I wanted it."

"As you had carefully planned. Well, if you are such good friends with her, how is it you don't know where she lives?"

"We always meet in public places except for the warehouse." Renee began exercising her arms by turn, doing yoga stretches.

Mark followed her every move, unable to look away. "You might have had her tailed."

"Tried that. Didn't work. She's good."

"So she won't have you over, but tells you intimate details of her life and trusts you with her nitro."

She linked her fingers and stretched high, providing a delicious view of her breasts. Perfect. "What I'll be using is not nitro and it's as safe to handle as modeling clay." She extended her legs and pointed her toes, then began leg lifts.

She was making him crazy. And hot. He took a deep breath. "You won't be using the real stuff, of course."

She only smiled and wiggled her eyebrows. *The tease.*

He cleared his throat and changed the subject. "So how long have you been…remote viewing? Trying to control it?"

Renee relaxed her pose and began staring out the window, but seeing into her past. "I was about eight when I became aware of it. But ever since I could first remember, I'd have this small space of time, right between sleeping and waking, when I seemed to be somewhere besides my bed. One morning, I hovered there, suddenly excited about having waffles for breakfast."

"Yes, I could see how that would fire you up. I suppose you 'saw' the plate waiting for you."

"No, I saw hands preparing the waffle iron, plugging it in, spraying the grids. I knew it was my mother and she was about to make my favorite meal. I woke up then and tore downstairs, eager to eat. It was just as I'd envisioned. The appliance was there, ready, and she was breaking an egg into the batter."

Mark watched her sigh. "Where is your mother now?"

"Teaching junior high in Florida. She was almost always my outbounder at first, probably because I loved her more than anyone else. When I first realized what I could do, I felt really good that I'd always know where she was and what she was doing as soon as I woke up every day. But gradually, I began to wonder if I could also see other people in the same way. So I tried my dad. It worked. Then my teacher." She laughed. "Got a really good education there!"

"Don't tell me. You caught her in bed." He made a face. "That's sort of sick, isn't it?"

She laughed again. "Let's just say it sure did hold my interest." She sobered then. "I experimented with the viewing and found out that I could choose the person. I'd think of someone just before I went to sleep and wish that I could be with them the next morning. It seemed to work most of the time. It took a while for me to discover that I couldn't use people I hated. They simply wouldn't appear."

How interesting. Had she wanted to be with him this morning? "And at other times of the day it didn't work?"

"It's very hard to get in the zone. Has to be that state of half-consciousness. I think the subconscious is more open then. Sometimes I can pick up a clue at odd moments, but it's unreliable. Only slightly more helpful than a shot in the dark guess." She resumed her isometrics.

"I see. And how did the government pick up on this talent of yours?" He deliberately ignored her provocative pose since he was fairly sure it was unintentional.

"I was working for the Secret Service at the time.

The recruitment was little more than a rumor making the rounds. One of my coworkers bragged that he had a little telepathic ability. Turns out he really did. We talked about it and he had the information and number to call. The rest is history. Not long after I went through the battery of tests they provided, I was offered the position where I work now."

"Using your unusual skill," he guessed.

"It's not listed in my job description. But, yes, I have used it on the job. We function as a civilian ops team working to prevent terrorism in any way we can. Any advantage we have, we use."

Mark rolled his eyes. "Well, we could sure use a couple of telepaths on this mission. Call in your troops."

She got up and began to pace. "You have to understand that we're spread pretty thin. There are only a few of us and there are other things going on in the world that require attention. This prevented kidnapping I'm investigating is not the highest priority. The planned bombing here might raise the op's importance, but in order for that plan to be realized, I would have to put the explosives in place. That, of course, won't actually happen."

"So you'll keep this going until you have the matériel in hand and discover where they come from?"

"Right, we need to track that source for sure. And of course, I need to try to identify who's in charge and anyone else who might be connected in any way.

"We want them *all* and we want them red-handed, every last one of those involved in this cell. Maybe that will include John Trip, too. You proved he's been in touch with Deborah and suspect that he's here. I've verified it for you. If they're merely lovers, he might not be involved in the planned attack, but maybe he'll tag along out of curiosity or something."

"I can't depend on maybes. I need to find him first, before you come down on the rest."

"And spook the others? Absolutely not! I can't let you jeopardize my op, Mark. Not for personal revenge against one man." Hands on hips, she looked prepared for battle.

He made a placating gesture. "Settle down. I won't wreck your mission." Something else occurred to him. Perhaps she didn't have the final say in how things went down. "You're not working alone, are you?" he guessed. "There's the guy that planted the car bomb, the one you got a photo of for Martine, right?"

She ignored his questions. "Maybe you'll get lucky and catch Trip on the way in or out of her place."

"We can set up surveillance," Mark suggested. "Real surveillance, that is. Unless you only want to check in every morning via brain satellite."

"Cute," she intoned with a disgusted look. "You're already messing up my waves. I didn't exactly choose you to outbound for me this morning, you know."

"So I guess you like me a tad more than you do ol' Deborah?" he asked with a grin.

"Marginally," she admitted wryly.

"So what do you admire about me most?" he asked, enjoying the byplay more than he should. She looked bothered a bit now. Good.

"You have an exceptional butt," she retorted, surprising him with her candor. "Guess that's why my subconscious followed it without my permission."

He shrugged and smiled. "What can I say but thanks?"

"Well, don't feel too smug just because I recognize your best feature."

Her playful teasing relieved some of the tension Mark was feeling. He would try to take his cue from her and keep things light.

Mark went out for a while and searched for the nearest store selling notebook computers. Renee had one, but he needed his own. The rest of the evening he spent completing his security plan and studiously avoiding looking at Renee any more than he could help. Bedtime was approaching.

They ate sandwiches he bought back, shared a couple of beers and said a perfunctory good-night. Judging from the sparse conversation, Mark figured she thought as he did. They had shared a bit too much personal information today, went a bit too far flirting and needed to back off.

This thing between them, whatever it was, couldn't be allowed to flourish. Nothing in that but a kick in the heart.

* * *

Renee awakened before dawn since she had made such an early night of it. It was rare for her to come fully alert the minute she opened her eyes. She usually drowsed, hoping for a vision. But she had smelled coffee brewing and that had done it for her.

She got up, dressed quickly and went out to find Mark sitting at the small table in the kitchenette. His new laptop sat open in front of him, a half-eaten croissant and a full stoneware cup to one side of it.

She helped herself to the coffee. "How's it going?" she asked conversationally, sliding into the chair opposite him, tucking one foot under her.

"Good and not so good. The security breach for the building is finished. But a contact at the local police assures me they have no murders reported in the city utilizing Trip's MO. At least not in the past couple of weeks."

She was fully aware that Mark had disappeared for several hours last night after she had gone to bed. Though he'd been perfectly silent, she had awakened just after midnight and gone for a glass of milk. The chaise had been vacant, as well as the pallet he had made on the floor. The bathroom door stood open and the room was dark. She had checked it anyway. She lay awake for a long time, thinking maybe he'd only gone outside to make phone calls so he wouldn't wake her. She never heard him return.

Well, he had his contacts to make and she had hers. Her people wanted a face to go with Mark's name so she needed to present him somehow without actually introducing them. She formed a plan as he talked and plunked idly at his new keyboard.

"Trip's a ghost. No chance that he's been spotted. I'm the only one who can put a face to his name." He smiled. "You obviously can, too, but you should be safe since he can't know that."

"You copied my drawing and passed it to your people, didn't you?"

He nodded. "I'm sorry if you mind that, but it was necessary. There's no other likeness of him. Your good mates Deborah and Sonny have seen him in person if your little vision was on the mark. I wouldn't give great odds on their survival when he's finished his business with them." He toasted her with his coffee cup. "Unless you get them first, of course."

"I will," she said. "And you'll get *him*, too." She grinned. "Got a feeling."

He closed his computer, braced his elbow on the table and looked out the window. "A feeling," he repeated, then met her gaze and raised his eyebrows. "So what sort of feeling do you have about today? I take it you had no revelations upon waking this morning."

"Nope. None." She grinned, reached for the remainder of his croissant and popped it into her mouth. "What I do feel is that we should take a break. The intensity of all this can impair judgment if we don't relax a little now and then. You've done all you can to find your man, and we do know where he'll turn up eventually. Both of us have completed the tasks Deborah set for us, so there's nothing more to be done at the moment but wait for the next step. You don't play much, do you?"

"What would you like to play?" He idly traced the edge of the table with his finger, drawing her attention to his hand, that supremely capable, well-trained, rather magic hand that could probably bring worlds of pleasure. The hand that could also kill. A beautiful weapon.

"Not games. Just play. You know, go out and have fun. After all," she said, gesturing to the window, "this is Paris. Have you been here many times before?"

He nodded, picking up a few stray crumbs with his fingertip and depositing them onto his plate. "A few."

"How many?" she pressed, simply to gather a few more facts about him. He was a fascinating man. A real enigma. There was a boyishness hidden beneath that forbidding exterior. She caught tantalizing glimpses of it now and then but not often enough.

"Paris is just a city like any other." His lazy smile held a dare.

She bit. "Are you kidding? Have you ever been to the Louvre? Now that's an impressive sight. Or acres of sights, I should say. You like art?"

He cocked his head. "So many questions, one would think you're an investigator! Suppose I said no."

"Well, you *will* like it." She stood up, reached down and grasped his hand. "C'mon, stick-in-the-mud. We're going to sightsee. I bet you've never even been up the Eiffel Tower. We could have lunch there!"

Grudgingly he got to his feet. "I've seen Notre Dame."

She pinned him with a baleful glare. "Huh, from the outside. Now give it up and come with me. You need a dose of culture and I need an art fix."

"Crikey, are all you Yanks hyperactive? Take your meds!"

She laughed. "Insults won't save you, lazybones. You are going to see Paris with me."

Stunned, he stopped in his tracks. "Don't say this is your first time!"

"No, but I haven't really done the tourist thing since I was about twelve." She tugged on his hand with both of hers. "Pretty please?" She really needed him to go, but didn't want him to know why. Not that she didn't trust him, but he really didn't need to know she was giving her people an opportunity to further check him out.

"Fine, I'll come with you," he agreed grudgingly. "But it's too far to walk in the cold."

"We can take the car. I'll drive." Renee almost giggled when his eyes widened.

"I'd rather jog barefoot the entire way," he declared.

They exited the apartment building and strolled toward Pont au Double, arm in arm, bundled in their jackets, their boots scuffing over the centuries-old cobbles.

"This is rather nice," he admitted eventually, smiling down at her.

They passed a group of obviously American tourists snapping pictures. "Want a group shot?" Renee asked them, then noted their horrified stares. She had forgotten how she and Mark were dressed. Parisians wouldn't blink, but these middle-aged, middle-America moms and pops must be wondering where the Hells Angels' bikes were parked. They held their cameras and purses to their chests and stuttered their no-thank-yous.

Mark threw back his head and laughed out loud. Even when she urged him out of earshot of the tourists, he couldn't quite contain it. It was the first time she had really seen him let go that way. "So glad you're amused. Jeez, I feel like a leper."

"Well, I think you look smashing, though your hair does frighten me a bit."

"My hair! What's wrong with my hair?" She feigned outrage.

He shook his head, wrapped his arm around her and hugged her close. Fairly well numbed by the cold at that point, they continued on their way.

Renee enjoyed watching Mark unwind. She had a sneaking suspicion that he had suppressed the boy inside him for entirely too long, almost long enough to destroy the fellow. She meant to resurrect him if she could. Life was way too short to spend it avoiding all joy. Sure, their missions were made up of serious stuff requiring intense dedication. But what were they saving the world for if not to enjoy it now and then?

They agreed they hated the ultramodern glass pyramid Mitterand had stuck in the courtyard of the Louvre, then entered through it to see the treasures housed in the old stone wings. "There's not enough of a transition," she stated, frowning at the sleekness of the new forced on the old.

"I suppose one either loves or hates it. No middle ground. Maybe that's the point. No middle ground."

"Well, I just don't get it," she insisted, shaking her head.

Mark tolerated her lingering inside the museum even though she had promised him the short tour: Venus de Milo, Winged Victory, a couple of her favorite old masters and, of course, the Mona Lisa.

"Experts are saying now that she was either a new mom or pregnant," Renee informed him. La Giaconda had always fascinated her.

He pursed his lips and squinted at the painting encased in protective glass. "Could be indigestion."

Renee slapped his arm. "There is no educating you. So what would *you* like to see?"

He sighed. "Food. I'm starved." He took off and she had to hurry to catch up with his long-legged stride.

"Let's find the bookstore. I want to get a map."

In the shop, Renee pondered her selection and hung around exploring until she spied an exquisitely dressed, petite, dark-haired woman approaching. Vanessa Senate.

They didn't trade glances or indicate in any way that they knew each other. Renee picked up a couple of brochures to go with the map guide and went to the cashier to pay. Vanessa chose several postcards with pictures of paintings as she openly ogled Mark. Hey, any woman would, Renee admitted.

Apparently oblivious, Mark kept his back to Vanessa as he studied a coffee mug with scenes of Paris. Then he returned it to its shelf and left the shop to wait outside for her. Vanessa followed, probably to get a better look, maybe even get a photo of him for their files.

Renee took her time. When she exited, Mark was waiting and Vanessa was nowhere to be seen.

Cat and mouse games. Who says we don't *play?* Renee thought with a sigh.

It had grown late, so they saved the Eiffel Tower for another day and walked back to her apartment. It had begun to rain just as they arrived.

"Thank you for a lovely day," she said when he closed the door behind him.

"Thank you for the art history lessons," he replied. "You should be hanging there one day. Your drawings are far better than some I saw today."

She laughed. "There speaks a trained expert! What is your specialty, sir?"

"Stick figures," he admitted. "I do the best damned stick figures you'll ever see outside the Pompidou." Then he raised that left eyebrow again.

"Did your friend get what she was after? I tried to present what you say is my best side."

Renee rolled her eyes heavenward, threw up her hands and laughed. She should have known.

Mark loved her laughter, the way the eyes glowed with mischief, the way she reached out and touched, even without physical contact. He realized he had never had the opportunity to see the real Renee until today.

"You were a happy child," he guessed as he flopped down on the chaise and patted the seat beside him.

She sat. "I was. Still am." She cocked her head and studied him. "And you weren't. All that stiff upper lip stuff, eh? *No messing about, Markie. Wouldn't do to grant the peasants a smile. They might expect, what? A regular bloke?*" She aped a British accent, though not too well.

He chuckled. "Wrong. I had a marvelous time with my mates, Tom and Hugh. My school was just down the street from home. Almost every weekend, my dad and I did something together. Fishing, boating, trips to the London zoo, yearly vacations to the seashore." He had almost forgotten those special times. "My mother had a marvelous sense of fun as well. She doted on me. I missed her enormously when she died. I was six. My dad did everything in his power to compensate."

"But then you lost him, too." Her steady voice

betrayed none of the compassion evident in her eyes. She took his hand in hers. "And you went into the system."

The system? "No, that's just spy background stuff. My dad did die but it wasn't like that at all. My father's partner saw after my education. I served in the army, worked a bit for SIS, then settled with Lazlo."

Her eyes narrowed on him. "Is working for him what beat the joy out of you, or was it obsessing about Trip?"

"I'm hardly obsessed," he argued. Lied, actually. He had to admit it had governed his every action since he was thirteen. And she was spot-on about the joy. Until he came to know *her*.

How long had it been since he'd laughed with someone? And had he ever felt this sort of sweet intensity, this compelling need to give or please, to make love instead of merely engaging in sex? Not until Renee.

"Perhaps you're right," he said, then smiled at her. "I think you must be a witch." He slid his hand across her abdomen, grasped the curve of her waist and squeezed. "And you have mesmerized me, you wicked Wiccan, made me your slave."

She giggled and squirmed, revealing her ticklishness as she pushed at his hand. "So stop, slave! I order you to stop!"

He goosed her unmercifully, their laughter a bawdy chorus until he rolled, landed on top of her and braced on his elbows. Silence fell as he looked down into her eyes. Those marvelous whiskey eyes. "Love me," he whispered and lowered his mouth to hers.

Her gasp of surprise stoked his determination, his imperative need to taste her, to have her. She succumbed. No, more than that. Her lips opened eagerly, welcomed him like a long lost lover.

"All kinds of reasons why we shouldn't…" she muttered against his mouth. Then she kissed him again, even more hungrily. He ignored her protest because it wasn't really that. Couldn't be. Merely stating the obvious before she grasped a handful of his shirt and tried to tug it away.

He slid one hand beneath her top, caressing her, kneading the firm muscles beneath the silken skin. *More,* his greedy mind demanded, the only word that would form. It erased everything else and grew in intensity until he could barely control himself. Or her.

Her hands were everywhere, seeking, finding, wanting as much as he wanted. Mark groaned with pleasure, a demand she answered.

Her fingers threaded through his hair, grasping, urging. She arched into him, raised her hips, cradled him…

A chirping sound invaded. *Her phone.* She collapsed beneath him, breaking the kiss with a harsh, impatient sigh as her hands slid from his hair. *No, damn it, no!*

He groaned again, this time in resignation, not even bothering to suggest she let it ring. She was already flailing one hand in the direction of the end table where the damned thing lay.

"Thank God!" She huffed almost angrily as her fingers closed around the little phone, fumbling until she had a grip on it.

Reluctantly he moved off of her and sat up, allowing her space to answer the call.

Judging by her heartfelt mutter at the untimely interruption, her response to the kiss had stunned her as profoundly as it had him. But the mood was broken and he knew he hadn't a prayer of getting it back now. Maybe not ever. She'd be on her guard and so should he, now that they both saw how easily they could get carried away.

She would say it was for the best they had gotten interrupted. Maybe it was.

But even knowing that, his hands clasped together as if they had the caller's neck between them.

Chapter 7

Mark had gone out before Renee finished talking with Deborah on the phone. Obviously frustrated, he had left without even grabbing his jacket. He didn't return until after she had gone to bed.

She heard him and expected he might attempt to pick up where they'd left off. Fully prepared to fend him off and explain why they had to keep things platonic, she couldn't help the sharp sting of disappointment that followed her into sleep.

This morning, he appeared to have forgotten anything had happened. He hadn't made even the slightest reference to it, oblique or otherwise. She decided to follow his lead. Surely they both realized what a mistake it would have been.

He readily accepted her suggestion that they go out, probably for the same reason she'd made it. Being cooped up in the apartment was not a good idea. They needed to get away from any place that had a bed in it. Or any privacy. Hell, they really wouldn't even need a bed....

Renee sighed with frustration. Why couldn't she have him? She argued against her better judgment. Who would it hurt? They were both adults. Consenting adults.

It could hurt her, of course. And maybe him, too. Nothing could come of it but a bout of mind-rending sex. Okay, maybe more than one bout. But it would be a temporary connection at best. Oh, but she had no doubt it would be the best.

She was afraid that she was getting too close to Mark in other ways for sex to be enough. If she got any closer, leaving him might break her heart.

The dichotomy that was Paris was never more apparent than in the early morning rush hour, she thought. They crossed out of the fifth arrondissement and headed toward Champs Elysées and beyond to the seventeenth, to Rue de Courcelles. She wanted to see the place where Mark thought Deborah lived and make certain it was the one in her vision before she called in a surveillance crew.

Deborah had called last night to check on the work Renee was doing and she'd assured her all was progressing nicely. Renee hoped she hadn't sounded too curt or unappreciative. That only proved how dangerous it was to get involved with Mark. She couldn't keep a clear head around him. All the warnings she'd gotten in training about interpersonal relationships with a partner on the job made perfect sense.

She tried to dismiss the whole incident from her mind and concentrate on her surroundings. It was still early morning. Pedestrians ambled along to work while motorists honked, gestured and flew around one another in a dedicated game of get there first.

"Can't help but love this place," she muttered, chuckling and pointing at a compact car bumping a parked one a few feet forward to create an extra space.

"You liked living here," he guessed.

"I liked living everywhere we went," she admitted. It was as if she couldn't keep her big mouth shut around him. That deep, mellow, secrets-in-the-dark voice of his just invited confidences, intimacy.

Right on cue, he asked, "Where did your family go after your time in Paris?"

She shrugged off the question. He was getting entirely too personal. No point in her being a motormouth. "We lived all over."

"Living here explains your excellent French." He kept pushing for details and Renee didn't appreciate that. They passed a small café. "You want to stop for coffee?"

Before she could answer, her phone chirped. She needed to change it to music or something. The sound of it was beginning to grate on her nerves. She flipped it open. *"Oui. Certainment. Dix heure? Bien."* She clicked off and looked up at him. "That was Sonny. We're to meet them at Café Rouge at ten."

He glanced at his watch. "Half an hour."

"It's that way, across the bridge. Easier to walk than try to find the metro, but we'll have to hustle to make it in time. I'll have to verify the building another time." She reversed their direction and led the way.

"Wonder what's up?" he asked, matching his stride to hers.

"Who knows with Deborah? Everything's a test of some kind." She gave a little grunt of exasperation. "She's calling the shots, but I'm not sure what to think of Sonny. He gives this big, dumb jock impression most of the time, but then I'll see this cagey expression in his eyes, almost as if he's letting her do her thing and just monitoring. What do you think?"

"I think Sonny's smarter than he lets on, but my vote still goes to her as the power."

"Is Lazlo running a check on her?" Renee asked. "I've got my people on it."

"Nothing to run with. If you've got photos, I could use some."

Renee shook her head. "None on Deborah. Hard to catch her unaware. I did do a sketch. I'll get that for you and see if you have better luck with your sources. Sonnegut's pic we have on file. So far all we have on him is the attempted kidnapping and the killing of the two Secret Service agents."

"Thanks. Also, you need to clue me in on your plans and be specific."

"I plan to do exactly what Deborah instructs me to do. For now. You're to do the same. No questioning her motives. No making alternate suggestions. Got it?"

"You're the boss," he snapped. "For now," he added, repeating her words.

She stopped and grasped his arm, stopping him. "For the duration of this mission. I can have you removed if you interfere."

"And I can *remove you* if necessary," he warned.

"You'd get rid of me just to have your revenge on one man?" She didn't believe he would, but the coldness in his eyes made her wonder if her assessment might be a little off.

"Come on, let's go." He started walking again, his long stride eating up the sidewalk so efficiently, she almost had to run to keep up.

"Look, I'll help you get this guy, Mark. You trust me, don't you?"

He laughed and sighed. "Trust is a commodity I very seldom deal in."

"Yeah, me, too, but we *have* to trust each other on this," she insisted. "You know we do."

"Just like that," he stated, snapping his fingers.

"No, not *just like that.* I've put my life in your hands, telling you as much as I have. You've done the same thing. Weird as it feels, we don't have any choice but to trust."

"Hard to put much faith in someone who threatens to *remove* you, isn't it?"

"I didn't mean *kill* you, Mark, just that I could get you out of the picture if I needed to. There are other ways."

"Yes," he agreed. "And I know them all, *bébé*. Keep that in mind."

The Café Rouge seemed a strange choice for a meeting since it apparently offered no privacy. The tables outside were filled, mostly with tourists. Inside, what little seating there was was taken. Mark ushered Renee to the bar and elbowed out standing room. Before they could order anything, a waiter appeared and beckoned.

Renee followed the boy and Mark fell in behind her as they threaded through the tables to a door in back. Outside, there was a small courtyard with an awning. Deborah and Sonnegut sat there drinking wine and sharing a plate of crepes.

"Ah, the lovers appear at last! You're late," Sonnegut said with a boisterous cackle and a pointed look at his Rolex knockoff. "Two whole minutes!" He winked at Mark. "You a two-minute wonder, Alexander?"

Mark shrugged. "On a very good day."

More laughter. Even Martine joined in, sounding as if she'd had one too many glasses of wine. "What do you say, Renee? Is he up to your standards?"

"Quite," Renee said with a grin. "How are the crepes, edible?"

"Delicious! Sonny and I ordered veal liver. They cook it to pink perfection here. You must try it."

They did as she suggested, though Mark thought it was more a directive than a suggestion. The woman irritated him with her sly glances and catty innuendo. And that devilishly illusive sense of familiarity. He had seen her before, he was sure of it. But where and when?

He went with the flow, waiting to see what developed next. For over an hour, they did nothing but enjoy the cool sunny morning, adequate food and excellent wine. They might have simply been two couples meeting for brunch with nothing more important to discuss than the latest cinema or the rising price of petrol. But beneath the banalities there lurked a dark undercurrent of hidden meanings.

Suddenly Sonnegut pushed away from the table and stood up. "I am going to stretch my legs." He looked at Mark. "Come, we'll take a walk."

Mark rose and threaded his way back through the café behind the man. When they were outside, Sonnegut lit a cigarette and offered the pack to Mark.

Declining with a shake of his head, he waited.

"So what have you found?"

Mark shrugged. "She's given me no reason to believe she's other than she claims to be. Most of the time's been spent working on the project. Seems industrious."

"Has she made any phone calls?"

"Only once. She tried to reach Deborah to ask her a question about something on the plans."

"Excellent. And what is she like in bed?" he asked with a grin.

Again Mark shrugged. "Agreeable enough." He didn't want to give Renee a great recommendation there. Sonnegut might want to sample her himself.

"Ah, not too adventurous, eh?"

"She'll do for now," Mark said and pointedly changed the subject. "Can I expect to stay on after this job's completed?"

"Perhaps," Sonnegut said and flicked his cigarette out into the traffic. "I will recommend you if you make no mistakes."

"Thanks," Mark said sincerely. Sonnegut had just answered one of their primary questions. He was *not* the one making the decisions. "Shall we rejoin our ladies?"

The movie Martine was critiquing as they returned to the table had a theme entirely too similar to the diabolical plans they were putting in motion.

"This plot point in the film, I would change," she announced, interrupting herself with a noisy slurp of wine, then pointing at Renee with her glass. "The protagonists should see things through to the end instead of dashing off to the airport, don't you think? By running, they encouraged chase. Also they never got to view the results of all their careful plans."

"Ah," Renee said, nodding. "Good points."

"Precisely!" Martine exclaimed. "You agree?" She lasered the question on Sonnegut who was pouring her yet another glass of wine from the carafe.

"Whatever you say, my heart. But I do believe the film runs on too long. A shorter time frame would heighten the impact on the audience."

"I don't know," Renee said, playing along with them. "Drawing out the suspense might be the wiser move in this case. Give everyone time to grasp every aspect of what is to happen."

Martine sat up straight and plunked her glass down so hard, wine sloshed into her plate. She leaned forward, unsmiling now, and shook her spread fingers at Renee. "Five days."

Renee shot Sonnegut a look to mark his reaction, but said nothing.

Mark bit his tongue to keep from arguing. Renee must realize, too, that there was no wiggle room here. He had five days to find Trip if he was to be found. Once Renee and her team lowered the boom on Martine and Sonnegut, Trip would disappear again.

Unless he was involved in the actual execution of the plan. If that were so, Trip would be gathered up with all the others. Or shot dead at whatever scene was planned. Mark meant to get to him first. But somehow he had to do that without damaging Renee's overall plan.

Whether she believed him or not, Mark did see the bigger picture. These people had to be stopped and there couldn't be any remnants of the group left to reorganize themselves.

The only way to keep from scotching Renee's op by taking Trip out first was to catch the man alone and not alert the others.

"We should go now," Deborah said, again wearing her tipsy smile as she beckoned for the check. "I am expecting a courier to deliver the package later this afternoon. I wouldn't want to miss it."

Renee pushed her chair back and prepared to leave. "Will we see you again soon?"

"Let's do this again the day after tomorrow, eh?" Sonnegut said, bonhomie oozing from every suntanned pore. "We will call you with the time and place."

He reached for Renee's hand and brought it almost to his lips. *"Au revoir,"* he said with a chuckle and a wink at Mark.

Mark managed to air kiss both sides of Deborah's face in the expected farewell salute.

Renee didn't have to guess what Sonny had said to Mark. Deborah had grilled her thoroughly in their absence. It was definitely as suspected. She and Mark were set to observe and report on each other, to insure one another's dedication to the effort. "Have you noticed we're all traveling in pairs on this thing?" Mark asked as they left the café, almost as if he had read her mind. "Even when Sonnegut was detailed to make those calls about me, she saw to it that Beguin stayed with him. Then there's the other couple of musclemen. I'll bet they run together as well. Seemed fairly chummy. Probably following us right now.

"Sonnegut said he'd recommend me if I did a good job. That means he doesn't have the final say. Also, that decision about the time frame had already been made and they weren't even willing to discuss it. That tells me someone else made that call and they had orders."

"Maybe whoever is running this show paired Deborah with Sonny. Or Deborah could have decided it and was simply being bullheaded." Renee blew out an exasperated breath and shook her head. "I have to find out. And soon."

"Well, even though she thinks you saved her life, Martine doesn't trust you out of her sight."

"Apparently not." She'd just been thinking that Deborah would surely send someone with her to set the charges. Someone in addition to Mark, though he would have to be there, too, to get them past security.

"I wonder who Trip gets to party with. Unless…"

"He's the boss," Renee said, completing Mark's sentence.

"It's impossible to tell whether Deborah made the decisions, or if she's merely following orders."

"But maybe not Trip's," Renee said. "You said he's only a gun for hire."

"Yes, but suppose he's branched out. He has been at the top of his game for some time now. Shooting people must get boring after a while, especially when your signature rarely varies."

"Serial killers never vary it, do they?" Renee had studied profiling.

"Ah, but Trip's not that. He's an assassin, not a thrill killer, though I imagine he enjoys his work. His signature has to do with pride, not compulsion. Most likely he uses it as a way to verify he's done the work himself so he'll get paid for it."

"Three shots to the head and he leaves his card? How stupid is that?"

Mark shrugged. "Hey, it's worked for him all this time. Free advertising and proof of results."

"And a guarantee that everybody and his brother will be after his butt. How is it he's managed to get away with it for so long?" Renee asked, feeling the tension in Mark's arm suddenly grow tight.

"Because I'm the only one who has seen his face to know who he is."

"Then why hasn't he gone after you?"

"Because he doesn't know I exist."

"You've seen him, but he's never seen you?"

Mark nodded but didn't reply. Renee saw his throat work and his jaw tighten as he relived the memory. She suspected who the victim had been, so she didn't push for details. The need for vengeance radiated from him like heat.

"We should stake out Deborah's place," she suggested. "If he comes back, we could follow him, find out where he's staying."

"Already done. I sent your drawing along with the approximate address to Lazlo. He's taking care of that. If Trip's spotted going in to meet with Martine, I'll be there to take him coming out."

Renee halted in her tracks. "No! If Trip disappears, the rest might abandon everything! We could lose them all!"

"You won't lose them," he promised. "Even if they scatter, I'll help you catch every last one of them. My word."

"Like you caught Trip?" she retorted, striking below the belt, she knew. "How long have you been after him, Mark?"

A long pause ensued. She didn't think he would answer her. Then he sighed. "Actively? Eight years and five months. I'd begun preparing for it long before that."

Renee gave a laugh of disbelief, but Mark looked very serious. Deathly so. "Not obsessed, huh?"

"He killed my father," Mark said without expression and walked on ahead.

Renee followed and caught up to him, but she didn't resume the conversation. No way would she ever convince Mark to wait on apprehending Trip. *Apprehending* was an optimistic thought and obviously not what he had in mind anyway. She could hardly blame him for it. If the man had shot *her* father, nothing on earth could stop her from squashing him like a bug the very first chance she got.

A cooler head than Mark's had to rule here. "Set

up a meeting with Lazlo for me. I think we need some face-to-face coordination." Surely Mark's boss could rein him in.

"No."

"What do you mean, *no?*"

"Just that." He refused to look at her and kept his strides long so that she nearly had to run to keep up. "Lazlo doesn't do meetings. You're not even supposed to know about him."

Renee switched tactics. "All right. Look, I need to get back to the flat. Are you coming?"

He nodded and followed her as she turned to cross the bridge to the Left Bank.

On the way across, he slowed his gait and reached for her hand. For show, she supposed. They were probably being followed, but no one was close enough to overhear them.

Mark might appear to be lost in his own thoughts, but Renee wasn't fooled. His peripheral vision was getting a workout, as was hers.

What she wouldn't give to be able to stroll down a street without feeling compelled to check the reflections in every store window she passed, or enjoy a glorious sunny vista without panning each potential place of concealment within the surrounding landscape. The continuous awareness was second nature to those in their line of work.

"See anyone?" she asked, wondering if his eye was as good as hers.

"Etienne, but he dropped us when we started

over the bridge. Knows where we're going. No point wasting man hours."

"That's good. I mean, that it was only him. I think we only have the six to deal with—Deborah, Sonny, Beguin, Piers, Etienne and Trip, of course. I haven't seen anyone else."

"Even in your morning visions?" he asked, but the usual sarcasm was missing. The bleakness in his eyes had faded now that she had distracted him from his memories.

"Nope, no one that could be involved.

"Have you tried at any other times of day or night?"

Renee nodded. "Not much luck, though. Once I tried using Piers as the outbound. I only saw a shrewish wife and a flat full of squalling kids. I was glad there was no audio on that one. At least he has a life outside the group."

"So you found something worthy enough in him that you could…connect?"

"I wouldn't say worthy, but he's not mean, just a schmuck trying to make money in a hurry. My guess is he grew up in the black market and it's all he knows."

"He's savvy enough to acquire explosives, quite a supply of them if he's the bloke in charge of *provisions*."

Renee smiled. "Well, we don't have them *yet*. Maybe he's not all that great at his job. That could give us the delay we need."

"Hope springs eternal," Mark muttered as they

neared her apartment building. "Here we are. Go on up. I think I'll pop down to the market and pick up something for dinner."

"You cook?" she asked, astounded. He simply didn't look the type to tie on an apron and stir pots.

"A little. I get sick of restaurants and I'm not big on French food."

Renee chuckled. "Didn't go for the duck liver, huh? I have to warn you, I'm not wild about bangers and beans, either."

"Or our famous black pudding? Not to worry."

He waved and was off.

Renee started up the stairs, drawing her weapon as she went, the clearing habit as ingrained as brushing her teeth in the mornings. Domesticity would take more practice than either if she ever got around to it. But watching a hard-edged English spy play Iron Chef should be interesting as hell. The very thought made her laugh. He'd probably open a couple of cans of soup and call it cuisine.

She kicked off her boots, changed into lounge pants and a pullover and got busy packaging the plans. When she had finished, Mark still hadn't returned. She called for the courier.

Renee toyed with the idea of following the guy to Deborah's place, but decided against doing it herself. Mark would be back soon anyway.

He knew where Deborah lived and said Lazlo had taken care of the surveillance there. But maybe it wouldn't hurt to put someone there she could count on to notify her of what was going on.

If Mark got word Trip was there, he certainly wouldn't share the information. No, he'd just take off and go get him.

She grabbed her cell phone and called Control. Preserving the mission was necessary. If Mark's vengeance got in the way of it, she would need to know immediately so she could arrange damage control. "I need eyes. How soon can you get a bike over here to tail a courier and then set up a stakeout?"

So much for partnership and trust.

Chapter 8

Mark brought dinner when he returned, not minding the effort it would take to prepare it, though he'd practically had to furnish the small kitchen with everything but the pots and flatware.

He watched her struggle with the head of lettuce, trying to pop the stem of it the way he had suggested. She wasn't much help. He figured her for a take-away sort and not that familiar with food preparation. He recalled his own days of paper-wrapped fish and chips and microwave dinners. "Give it a spot-on rap, then twist it out," he advised.

"Damn it!" She had smashed her finger in the process.

Mark put down the knife he was using to split the

filets and took over, neatly cored the lettuce and then took her hand in his. "Run some cold water over it." He stuck her fingers under the faucet and did it for her.

"Cooking sucks," she muttered, glaring down at the injured digit.

He raised her hand to his lips and took her finger into his mouth, caressing it with his tongue. She watched, holding her breath, then gave a nervous little chuckle.

Mark removed her finger from his mouth and then kissed it gently as he watched her eyes widen. Without pausing, he lowered his lips to hers and kissed them, too. Not the soul kind of kiss that he wanted, but one that might make her want more. Then he released her, turned off the faucet and handed her a towel.

She peered up at him, looking a bit disgruntled. "That's it?"

He laughed and shook his head. Putting her off balance was something he had seldom been able to accomplish. Even when he managed to, it usually backfired on him.

Would she want more? If she did, would he be able to give it? He had firmly decided he couldn't afford anything ongoing after they were finished here in Paris. He would have to disappear again and she would be an ocean away, doing what she did. The regret he felt at that troubled him more than he wanted to admit. He knew he had begun to care too much about her, about her feelings.

She cleared her throat and went back to the counter, turning her back on him. "So, how is it you learned so much about cooking? You strike me as a guy with a privileged upbringing, servants and all. I'm surprised you can boil water."

He smiled. "Privileged? By that you mean wealthy?"

She nodded. "I know what you told me about being middle class, but it's your accent. I'm very good at identifying them." She took up the lettuce and proceeded to tear it into pieces for their salads. "Upper crust. Fancy private schools, then Cambridge or somewhere like that. Am I right?"

Mark shrugged and went back to the filets, sliding the thin blade horizontally, expertly. He was good with a blade.

She pushed. "You don't get into those without family standing and money. *Lots* of money," she added with a knowing nod.

"We call them *public* schools. Yes, I went to Stowe, then Oxford."

"I knew it! You downplay the accent when talking to the others."

"I can do a right Cockney," he admitted, putting it on for emphasis, "but I thought that might be a bit over the top." He smiled at her. "My father was a public servant. Worked for the government. My mother was a homemaker, never wanted to be anything else, she said."

"An admirable goal," Renee said, looking quite sincere. "But none of that explains your accent."

"After they died, I had a mentor. I suppose he had an influence. At least he provided influence."

"Well, you were very lucky in that."

"Lucky?" he snapped, angered by her assumption.

"That you had someone who sent you to good schools, who cared enough—"

"Cared?" Mark had never felt anyone had cared since he'd lost his parents. Even Lazlo, who had taken him in, educated him for a purpose, had him trained to kill and expected payback with every breath Mark took.

He and Lazlo had a common goal, that was all. Lazlo had provided the skills for Mark to find his father's killer and demanded absolute loyalty and dedicated service in return. When Mark wasn't tracking down Trip, he worked the other jobs Lazlo threw him. Deep cover. Working alone.

Mark had gone to university, served his military obligation and completed his intelligence training using his middle name, Alexander, as his surname. That had died with his father, leaving no trace of the family Brevet. For Mark's protection, Lazlo had insisted on that. Trip was not one to leave loose ends lying about.

Maybe Lazlo *did* care a little, Mark admitted for the first time. Maybe he had saved Mark a brutal death at a very young age. In the years following his brief span at SIS, Mark had put himself at Lazlo's disposal, knowing from the outset that this was expected of him.

Lazlo had used him, true. But maybe he had done all he'd done to help him, too. Mark realized he would probably never know the man's real motive for sponsoring the orphan of his murdered partner. Most likely, there was no single reason, but several. Lazlo himself might not be able to answer the question in his own mind, much less explain it if asked. Not that Mark ever *would* ask.

"I suppose I was lucky," he admitted. "So…I've given up all my secrets. What about you?"

She grinned, happy now to have the salad conquered. "I lose mystery status if I tell."

"It's only fair," he replied, sneaking a sprig of lettuce from the bowl. "Your mates know who you are. Can't you consider me one now? You *were* the one promoting trust."

Her smile dwindled to a thoughtful look as she studied him for a minute. Then she took a deep breath and began. "I was home schooled for the most part since we were traveling all over. Occasionally I would attend one of the local schools so I could pick up the language. At seventeen, I went to a junior college in Florida. Last two years at Georgetown. Scholarship," she said proudly.

"Then you were with Secret Service and found your way into this unit you work for now?"

"That's it. Me in a nutshell."

"The real Renee Leblanc," he said quietly, wondering if he dared reveal his real name. Somehow, he wanted to share that secret with someone after all this time. As far as he knew, no one else was aware of who he was other than Lazlo, who had ceased to be a mentor years ago and was now merely his boss, a voice on the phone and a signature on his paycheck.

Renee dealt out two plates and rummaged through the silverware drawer. "What you see is what you get, unless I decide otherwise."

"My name is Brevet," he said on impulse. He surprised himself by giving in to the impulse. And surprised her, too, obviously. "Marcus Alexander Brevet," he added.

She looked stunned, standing there with a dinner fork in her hand. Then she released the breath she had sucked in and stepped closer. She touched his face, just a brush of her fingers. "Thank you for telling me, Mark," she said, almost in a whisper as her amber gaze fastened on his.

He wanted to kiss her so badly his teeth ached. Instead he clicked his tongue, turned away and popped the steaks into the broiler. "Don't bother looking me up under that. You won't find anything past age thirteen."

"I don't need to," she assured him. She hadn't moved. He thought she might kiss him, but she only smiled.

Well, there it was. He had given her all the ammunition she needed to destroy him if she wanted.

If she did look him up, she would find his father and all the details leading up to his murder. A suspected traitor, a man under investigation who had died on his kitchen floor. Murdered before he could gather enough evidence to exonerate himself.

Perhaps she'd find a small, insignificant notice that the son had simply disappeared immediately after the private funeral. Any lad with a shadow like that over his head would want to run away, wouldn't he?

Yes, maybe Lazlo had cared. And maybe he had saved Mark in more ways than one.

He wondered if he could trust the look on Renee's face at the moment. She looked like *she* cared. He had touched her with his admission and that was most likely his subconscious intent. He quite consciously wanted to touch her in every way imaginable, but giving her this measure of trust was the best he could do.

The meal went well. Incredibly so. "That was amazing! Absolutely worth risking mad cow disease. I almost never eat beef anymore."

Mark grinned as he reached for Renee's empty plate. "Well and truly done to a turn, as we English prefer, so you're quite safe."

"You qualify as a bona fide chef," she declared. "That's the best chateaubriand I've ever eaten. But it's still a French dish," she teased. "I thought you had an aversion to French food."

"Ah, but I've made it my own," he argued, pouring her another glass of wine. This evening she looked more like the woman he had met in Virginia. He liked the soft blue velour top and pants she had put on. And how she had forgone the hair gel and fluffed out her hair so that it lay in a wavy chin-length cap that invited caressing. He didn't do that, of course. The kiss earlier had been a risk. He shouldn't compound it.

He really shouldn't, he reminded himself yet again. Still, everything he'd done so far tonight seemed geared to pursue that risk.

"I can't have another glass of that," she said, eyeing the excellent red longingly. "One's my limit when I'm working."

"So I noticed at the café. Why don't you live a little? We haven't anything else to do tonight. Deborah and Sonnegut will be busy going over your work on the building layouts. I have surveillance covered. Nothing's going to happen for a while yet."

"What if Trip shows up to go over those plans with them? You hope to get me drunk enough that you can leave me here and go after him?"

"If keeping you here was my intention, I could always overpower you and tie you up."

She laughed and picked up the wine, taking a defiant sip. "You could always *try*."

He leaned forward, resting his arms on the table. "Look, I promise I won't jeopardize your plans if I can possibly help it. If I can take Trip when he's alone, they'll never know. Everything will go forward just as you hope."

"Unless he's the one directing traffic. They won't make a move without him if he is."

He sat back, toying with his wineglass, twisting the stem and staring at the burgundy liquid as if it were a crystal ball. "Can you promise me he'll be taken alive? And that he'll be turned over to us?"

She thought for a moment. "By *us*, you mean you and Lazlo?"

"That's right."

"You know I can't. Lazlo's not law enforcement. He's a private citizen with a private concern. Besides that, I won't be in charge when this goes down. Trip could very well be killed if he's with the others and resists arrest."

Mark had trusted her earlier with information that could threaten his existence. He had to give her more. "Renee, I need to talk to him. There are questions that need answers and he's the only hope we have of getting that information. We have to know who hired him."

"Does it have to do with your national security? If it does, you know you have channels you can go through." She paused only a moment, then added, "But it's personal, isn't it, Mark?"

"Not entirely." He puffed out a breath of frustration and raked his fingers through his hair. "Only on my part. It has to do with an investigation that was ongoing a number of years ago, one that involved both Lazlo and my father. They were accused of treason. My father had been gathering evidence to clear them when Trip killed him. Lazlo was arrested and tried. He soon escaped and proved his innocence, but the real culprit was never found. We must find out who wanted my father dead. Whoever hired it done is the real traitor."

She sat back, tapping a finger against her lips as she pondered what he'd said. "It was a long time ago, Mark. Your culprit could be dead by now." Then she shook the finger at him. "That's why Lazlo left SIS and started his own business, right?"

Mark had no right to speak for him though he knew it was true. "All I can say is that my father died under this shadow. He was dead—the perfect fall guy! And the real culprit goes free. I want his name restored."

"I don't blame you," Renee said thoughtfully. "I would want the same thing if I were you." Her eyes seemed to see right into his heart then. "You want to kill Trip yourself, don't you?"

Mark looked away. That, too, was true, but Mark had promised not to do it in exchange for Lazlo's help. God knew how much he owed that man. "Lazlo needs to question him, to find the one responsible for setting them up and then killing my father. Then…I suppose the authorities will deal with Trip."

Renee reached across the table and put a hand on his, just a light squeeze that felt so damn comforting. "I'll do everything I can to help you with what you and Lazlo need, Mark. I understand, I really do."

Her dratted cell phone chirped. Renee looked at the readout. "Deborah." The conversation was brief.

Mark watched her face as she clicked off. "She wants us to come *there* in the morning at ten. I can't believe she actually gave me the address!"

"What do you think it means? Did she give you any indication?"

Renee nodded, finishing her second glass of wine as her eyes held his. "She has someone she wants us to meet."

"Trip, you think?"

Renee set down the empty glass and sat back, crossing her arms. "Who else could it be? Will he recognize you?"

That question had occurred to him, too. "He's never seen me." But Mark knew that he strongly resembled his father. However, Trip had killed so many, he surely wouldn't remember all the faces. Even if he did suspect Mark's relationship to one of his victims, he couldn't be sure of it. "It's a chance we'll have to take. He can't know I was there and saw him that night."

Renee sat up straight. "What night? The night he killed your dad? You saw?"

"Not the actual shooting, but it was him, without a doubt. If dad hadn't alerted the police before he was shot and if they had not arrived straight away and scared him off, Trip might have found and killed me, too. He was as close as you are to me now."

"You were hiding?" she asked, then answered her own question. "Of course. You were what, thirteen?"

"Just. And I didn't know at the time that my father was dead in the other room. I thought he was hiding, too, since he had no weapon. He had turned over his service revolver while the investigation was ongoing."

"You're certain his murder had to do with that investigation?"

"Yes. Lazlo said my father had been making a defense for them, gathering data and putting it together. That was his specialty in SIS, connecting the dots. The file was missing from his desk and the only one who could have taken it was Trip. Much of the information was still in my father's head and he wasn't one to share, even with his partner, until he had something definite."

"And Lazlo was his partner," she deduced.

Mark nodded as he got up and began to pace, rubbing his fist with his hand, imagining it connecting with Trip's face, his gut. Tension had him wired to the max. He wanted to do something *now*, not wait until morning.

Renee rose, too, and came to him, halting him in his tracks. "Mark," she said, her voice soft yet firm. She placed her hands on his face, cradling it with her palms. "You have to stay with the plan. If Trip is there, you'll have to stay calm, not alert him in any way."

He knew she was right. "I can," he declared. "I will."

She raised up on her toes, drew his face down to hers and kissed him. Her motive was to calm him, distract him, and he knew that. But knowing it didn't stop him from kissing her back, almost vengefully, as if she were the one denying him his long held promise of vengeance.

She slid her hands around his neck and he embraced her fully, crushing her against him. Reasons for the kiss dimmed as heat flared through his body. The eager little sounds she made in her throat reverberated inside him, triggering his own sounds of need.

He lifted her without breaking the kiss and moved to the lounge, lowering her to the couch and coming down on top of her. "I want you," he gasped against her mouth and kissed her again to silence any protest. It angered him that he needed her so much, so desperately.

She should fight him, he thought. She should be afraid. Her fear was all that would stop him now. He couldn't bear causing her fear.

But she wasn't scared at all. In fact, she was tearing at his shirt. She curled one leg around his hips and pulled him more intimately into the cradle of her thighs, lifting to meet the rhythmic pressure of his body.

"Yes!" she hissed through her teeth and sought his mouth again. She tasted of wine and desire, delicious and mind-numbing desire that he had not felt since…ever.

Mark slid his hand between their bodies and yanked up her shirt. His fingers probed for and quickly found the snap on her bra. She raked his shirt aside and he felt her breasts pillow and flatten against his chest. He moved against her, loving the firmness of her curves, the sensation of skin against skin. His mouth took hers again and gave with a hunger different than any he had ever known.

He lifted his hips slightly as she unzipped his jeans and pushed them down. Her slacks followed and he felt her struggle to kick them off.

Without a pause, they came together in a hot rush of pleasure that stole his breath, stilled his heart for a moment that seemed a lifetime and yet was over too soon. Pure feeling took him. He pounded into her again and again, reaching for the path into her soul, her heart, her mind.

She clasped him with her arms, her legs, her body, arching into him, crying out his name, shuddering violently beneath him. The silken, tight heat of her was too much. He poured into her with everything that he was and ever hoped to be, a giving reserved for just this moment in time. Just for her. For them together. Mark sighed out what little was left of his soul and collapsed, out of breath.

She sniffled and buried her face in his neck.

Was she crying? He hadn't the energy to ask. Didn't really want to know. Of course, she was feeling regret already. A hasty tup in a run-down Parisian flat with a man she scarcely knew wouldn't be a girl's favorite dream. And they hadn't used any protection. A girl's worst nightmare.

He put one hand flat on the floor and pushed up a little so he'd stop crushing her into the stiff cushion of the couch.

"Tears?" he asked, feeling obligated to let her vent. Damn, what on earth could he say to make her feel better? He hadn't been gentle. He hadn't even been civilized.

"Don't worry about it," she said with a weak laugh. "Probably just relief."

"Relief? God, how can you say *that?* I'm… sorry, Renee."

Again, she chuckled, this time with real humor. "No, you're not."

"No," he admitted wryly, still a bit breathless. He shook his head, the fingers of one hand pressed to his temple. "I guess I'm not."

"I'm on the pill," she said. "Goes with the job."

"You don't need to worry about anything else," he promised her. "I'm in good health."

"Obviously," she said with a smile and snuggled against him, her wrists propped on his shoulders as he looked down at her. "I'd say you are absolutely in top form."

Mark grinned as he glanced along the chaise. "Not sartorially," he remarked, noting that she was wearing her top and bra up under her armpits and against her chin. Her tiny blue silk briefs still encircled one ankle. His shirt was half off, as were his jeans and he was still wearing his boots.

He rolled off of her onto the floor and handed

her the slacks she had discarded. Unsure what to say, he said nothing and merely began to set his clothes to rights.

"Look, don't beat yourself up about it, okay? Wasn't all your fault," she said. "This was inevitable. Hormones, adrenaline, enforced proximity."

She sounded so pragmatic about the whole thing, it bothered Mark. As if this would have happened to any two agents of the opposite sex who happened to be thrown together in a like situation. Casual sex, mutual satisfaction. Satisfied, he was, at least for the moment, but this had not been casual to him, not at all. He had never in his life experienced anything like it.

"No, you were using sex as a tool for distraction, to calm me down so I won't dash your mission," he grumbled, sure it was true, damning himself for trying to make this more in his own mind than it was to her.

"That, too," she admitted, her voice crisp and taut as a garotte. "So tell me, did it work?"

The anger was back. So was much of the tension, but it had nothing to do with Trip at the moment. "Quite effective," he declared with a firm nod, his back still to her. "Next time I know precisely what to request when the urge to kill comes over me."

"My, my, are we a little touchy?" she asked, a hint of laughter still there in her voice. "Would we rather have a declaration of love or something equally inane?"

He turned then and looked her square in the face. "Don't you believe in love?"

She laughed outright. "Sure I do! Okay, I'm madly in love with you. Happy now?" She held up one palm.

He grabbed her wrist. "Never say those words to me again unless you mean them."

"Are you saying *you* love *me?*" she asked, tugging out of his hold and sitting up, a smile still tickling her lips. "Get real."

"It's not something to joke about, that's what I'm saying."

"I never would have pegged you as a romantic." She sighed loud and long and stared out the window as darkness fell over the city of lights. "Romance. This is the place everyone believes is rife with it. People come here all over the world just to find it." She looked down at him sitting there on the floor. "In case you forgot for a minute, that's not why we're here, Mark."

He shrugged and got up, abandoning hope of any real connection with her. She wasn't ready. And, to tell the truth, neither was he. "Oh, *now* I remember," he said sarcastically.

"You're angry with me? Why are you angry?"

"I'm not," he lied. How could she dismiss what had happened between them as nothing but a reaction to their circumstances? Yeah, he was mad, but what could he say? No precedent existed in his past to help him out. Never had he felt this way about anyone.

He grabbed his jacket and slipped it on, tucking his weapon in the back of his belt. "Lock up after me. I'm going out for a while."

"Why? Where are you going?" She scrambled up, her legs and feet still bare. "Mark?"

He didn't answer because he didn't know. Something just told him that he needed to be away from her before he said more than he intended. Before she reduced what had happened between them to even less than she considered it now.

For her, it was sex, pure and simple. For him, he wasn't sure what it was, but there was nothing simple about it.

Maybe he was paying for past sins, all those times when sex had meant so little to him. What was it about her? He had sworn never to care deeply enough about anyone to make himself vulnerable to the pain of losing them.

So much for that vow. She had definitely sneaked in under his radar.

Mark walked out into the night, along the Seine, pausing now and then to watch the wave-chopped glow of lights reflected in the water. City of Light, Paris beckoned but offered him nothing compared to what he had left behind in Renee's cozy little walkup. He still wore her scent and it was driving him crazy. The memory of her soft skin against his wouldn't leave him alone. And he could still hear the rasp of her breathing as she came apart in his arms.

The crisp November air numbed his nose and ears, filled his lungs, yet did nothing to chill his heated thoughts of her.

He finally recognized the root of his fury and all the tension he still felt as he strode along the ancient path. *Fear.* For the first time since the night his father died, he felt afraid right through to his core.

The very mention of John Trip, and the thought of the assassin being in Renee's presence for whatever reason, terrified him.

Mark kicked at a loose stone and cursed his lack of control. Maybe Renee had bewitched him with powers she didn't even realize she had. The thought caused a bitter smile. "Little witch."

He had been unable to save his dad from Trip. What if the need arose and he couldn't save Renee either?

If it ever came to a choice between Renee's safety and the completion of his goal, Mark wouldn't hesitate to kill Trip on the spot. Maybe what disturbed him so much about his feelings for her was that his priorities had changed.

Were his loyalties changing as well? No, he could not let fear for her rush him into abandoning the posthumous promise he had made to his dad.

Since Trip was in Paris, a confrontation was almost inevitable at some point. If they encountered the assassin, Mark would have to find a way to stay between her and the threat.

* * *

In the Rue de Courcelles, Cassandra DuMont had a problem on her hands. Sonny's jealousy of John Trip had begun to trouble her more than it pleased her. It could interfere with her plans.

He was too possessive, as if she were a piece of property. As if she would ever belong to the likes of either him or Trip. Men. She should kill them all except for her son. And even *he* had begun to rebel.

"Let me handle things for you," Sonnegut said yet again, doing his best to sound tame and reasonable. She liked that, but knew he was acting. "We don't need this man. He asks for the moon, but I will do it for nothing!" He ran a finger down the curve of her shoulder. "Just for you, my sweet. A favor."

Cass tried to reason with him since she couldn't kill him yet. "I've known him a lot longer than I've known you, Sonny. We have a standing agreement, John and I. It's strictly business. Nothing personal," she said, rolling the building plans into a tight cylinder and stuffing them into a cardboard tube.

"Tomorrow, we go. You'll come along to help and to watch, but John handles the loose ends afterward. It is settled. I have made the call."

She saw Sonnegut clench his fists so he wouldn't hit her. God, but he wanted to, she could see it. He was beginning to lose all his charm and become very predictable. In fact, he was no longer of much use at all. John could fill all her needs from this point on. And he would take care of Sonny for her when he did the others. Cass doubted he would even charge her extra for his trouble.

Lazlo, however, would be hers to destroy, personally if she could arrange it. He had set the dogs on her when she was young and vulnerable and left her to suffer. He had killed her brother, caused her alienation with her father and ruined her life. Her wrath knew no bounds and she grew all hot and violent whenever she thought of him.

Lazlo would soon see what real power was. So would Sonnegut and his boys. Her son, she would take in hand the minute this strike at Lazlo was finished and she left Deborah Martine behind and became Cassandra again. Managing Trip was another matter. That man was the devil incarnate. The best she could do with him was execute a fair deal.

Sonny must have realized from her expression whom *he* was dealing with because he unclenched his fists and smiled his sweetest smile. "Anything you wish. You are the brains behind this, after all."

Her answering smile contained a taunt. "Convince me you're sincere, darling. And do make it good."

Chapter 9

Renee struggled for calm. She would not give Mark the satisfaction of knowing how badly he had hurt her feelings. They'd had the best sex in the world and then he acted as if she'd withheld something crucial. She wished to heaven she had. Like her stupid heart. She should know better.

Maybe then she wouldn't be feeling like the proverbial one-night stand this morning. "Well, you *are* that, aren't you?" she muttered to the mirror over the sink. "And you look the part." She added another lick of dark lipstick and tried on a sardonic smile. It fell sort of flat and looked sad.

Damn the man. Had she asked for anything? Had she demanded a commitment or railed at him for not using a contraceptive? No, she'd actually smiled and stretched like a cream-fed cat.

Oh, but she had wanted to stretch her arms around him, hold him to her forever and promise him anything he wanted. He had gotten to her big-time and not only with his pleasure-giving talents. Damn, she could see he needed someone to care about him, someone to love him. She had seen it two years ago. Maybe that's what drew her to him so strongly, his need for nurturing. What a joke. She didn't nurture. Anyone who knew her would vouch for that. He would probably laugh if he knew she'd had such weird thoughts about him.

But he'd been angry when she'd joked about love. That was what she figured he had expected her to do. Joke. What *did* he want from her anyway, a certified commendation on his fabulous performance?

Well, it *was* certifiable, that was for sure. *Enough!* She wouldn't spend another minute dissecting what had happened between them. Let him stew, but she wasn't going to.

She tugged the tube top down to display more cleavage. Her black nail polish needed a retouch, she noted, but didn't have time for it. And her cheeks were still too rosy, thanks to Mark's stubble. Another daub of chalky makeup fixed that. "There."

She came out of the bathroom, grabbed her black leather jacket and pulled it on, tucked her pistol in the pocket and went to face the music. To face him, and then Deborah Martine and her retinue of bad boys.

"Good morning," she snapped as she entered the lounge where he waited, sprawled on the chaise, his arms outstretched on either side.

"Ready?" he asked, not meeting her eyes.

So he was having a good pout. Typical male. What did he have to grump about? "Good to go," she replied, injecting false cheer into her voice. "Let's do this."

She didn't mention the possibility of his meeting John Trip, but knew that must be foremost in his mind. Maybe he was not pouting about last night, but worrying about this morning. As she *should* be herself.

She drove in silence as he gave curt directions to Deborah's apartment. Renee already had the address, both from Deborah and the agent who had followed the courier. It was the same as Mark had discovered, so at least they knew Deborah had some sort of semipermanent setup and wasn't hopping all over Paris to keep everyone confused.

They were greeted at the door by Sonnegut. He held out his hands. "Forgive me, but I must have your weapons. House policy."

They gave them up, all except the wicked blade Renee knew Mark wore concealed in his boot. Fortunately Sonny didn't frisk either of them.

"Thank you. Follow me," he ordered with a toothy smile.

Renee wondered if he bleached his teeth twice a day. They were blindingly white, perfectly straight and too large for his mouth. He wore a turquoise silk shirt unbuttoned to midchest and sported a solid gold chain. The brown leather pants looked painted on, revealing his pride and joy in near naked detail. There was a lot to be said about leaving some things to the imagination.

Amazing how cheap and showy Sonny looked in comparison to Mark in his understated and unrelieved black. But she was determined not to think about Mark in any context today except as a partner in the op. That's all she would allow him to be from now on, the surly jerk.

Renee hoped this wasn't a social call. Sonny looked entirely too pimplike for her peace of mind.

They entered the salon. Sonny definitely clashed with his surroundings. Everything here smacked of old money. Antique furniture done up in embroidered brocade stood accented with gilded lamps and paintings that appeared ancient and authentic. A medieval tapestry hung over an intricately carved rosewood sideboard that served as a bar. Cut crystal decanters and glasses sat ready for entertaining.

If Sonny clashed, Deborah fit right into the scene. She wore a gorgeous silk lounging outfit of muted gold that matched the highlights in her expertly tousled shoulder-length hair. Her makeup was perfect and subtle, not overdone as usual, and her accessories were few and probably priceless. The spiked heel sandals were also gold, studded with small amber stones.

Renee experienced a small pang of envy. The

woman definitely had taste to burn and had obviously been slumming with the group before. Today, her expression, her clothes and her surroundings radiated power *and* wealth. No one could fake a disguise like this unless born to it.

Who the hell *was* Deborah Martine and what was she really up to?

"Please, have a seat," Deborah invited in a sensuous, throaty drawl. She gestured languidly to the damask sofa across from her brocade-covered armchair. "Sonny, make us a drink, would you, love?"

Renee risked a look at Mark, wondering how he viewed the change in their hostess. Gone was the hard-edged power-tripping female who spoke with threat-tinged acerbity. She'd been replaced by a sultry yet dignified woman of means who would entice any man alive. Mark's gaze was locked on Deborah, but his expression revealed nothing of his personal reaction to her.

Sonny grinned suggestively as he handed Renee some sort of green drink served in a crystal highball glass. Mark got the same thing. Neither had been asked what they preferred. Their host returned the bar and brought a similar offering to Deborah. He held up his own drink as if to toast them silently.

"We have much to do," Deborah said, taking a healthy sip and sighing as if it were nectar of the gods.

Renee tasted hers. It was delicious, some sort of liqueur much like crème de menthe, only much,

much tastier. An after-dinner cordial for breakfast? Maybe Deborah's otherwise excellent taste didn't extend to proper drink etiquette.

"So what's our plan?" she asked, keeping her voice conversational. Wouldn't do to sound too eager to get on with things. According to Deborah's decision yesterday at the café, they had four days to go before setting things in motion.

"Let's finish our drinks first," Deborah said, flicking her hand toward the adjoining room. "Sonny, would you please make that call to our other guest?" Then, to Renee and Mark, she explained, "He'll be along shortly. I'd like you two to remain here at my apartment until everything else is in place. Any objections to that?"

Renee looked at Mark, who simply shrugged, then back at Deborah. "No, but if we're to be here several days, I'll need to pick up some things from my apartment." And make a few phone calls to alert the troops while she was at it. She couldn't risk that here. The walls probably had ears.

Deborah shook her head. "That won't be necessary. I'm sure I can provide anything you'll need. And it won't be for very long." She held up her glass. "A new liqueur I acquired from Greece. Isn't it wonderful? I call it ambrosia."

Renee returned her smile and took another swallow. What *was* this stuff?

Mark watched Deborah like a hawk until she had

polished off her own drink. Then he drank his, making a face as he finished. "Sweet," he commented.

"It's the honey," Deborah said. "Exquisite, isn't it?"

Renee nodded and sipped a bit more. The taste became cloying after a few minutes, so she simply held it.

"We will watch the building come down," Deborah said, glancing at the window as if she could see it now, even though it was a couple of miles distant in a suburb of the city. "I think we should all see it. A learning experience, eh? You've chosen a place that's out of danger yet close enough for a good view?"

"Yes, I noted it on the plans. The building under construction, less than a block away." Having them all together in one group would be perfect. Whoever was directing the show would certainly be there. She couldn't have hoped for a better scenario.

She noticed her mouth felt dry, but she didn't want any more of the sticky sweetness of the so-called *ambrosia*. Food would be good. She hoped Deborah would provide it soon. They hadn't had breakfast. Her mind drifted as the faint sound of music floated around her. Ravel? No, it was…no matter.

Renee turned her gaze to the doorway where Sonny had disappeared to make the call. Was the guest already here? Was it Trip? There was no sound at all except for the music. No voices, nothing but that faint orchestra playing…what was it?

Mark reached over and grasped the hand she had rested on the cushioned seat between them. He squeezed it as if warning her of something. She looked over at him to see if he'd give her a clue.

His face wavered like a film out of focus. For a moment, she thought a vision was coming on, but no, it wasn't that. Her limbs hung like lead weights. Mark's hand relaxed its grip completely, but remained in place over hers. The light in the room dimmed.

Suddenly panicked, realizing she had been drugged, Renee shifted her gaze to Deborah and saw her smile widen.

"Don't worry, darling. You have done your work well. Now you can rest a while." Deborah's voice drifted away with the light and the music.

Renee's last muddled thought was that they would probably rest forever, but she hadn't the energy left to care very much. Mark would be so mad…

"Wake up!" Renee snapped, shaking Mark's shoulders and slapping his face none too gently. She had come to in a bedroom, lying on a satin counterpane, stretched out like a corpse with her hands folded over her chest.

Mark lay on the carpet, an oriental that had enough age and sheen on it to be worth a damn fortune. That indicated they were still at Deborah's. At least the decor was much the same.

Unfortunately they would probably be here a while. Renee had discovered the door locked and the windows painted shut. They were two stories off the street, an alley, really, with no traffic.

Mark grunted and idly batted at her hands. Obviously he'd had more of the drug than she had. She shook him again and his eyes opened a mere slit. "Wha…?"

"Wake up. They drugged us. God only knows what she and Sonny are up to. I tried to focus on her as soon as I came around, but I got nothing. We're locked in. And they took the cell phones."

He struggled, groaned and tried to sit up. She tugged on his shoulders to help.

"What's going on?" he mumbled, scrubbing his hands over his face and giving his head a few sharp shakes.

Renee repeated what she'd just said as she lifted one of his eyelids and checked his pupils. Still dilated, but they contracted when she turned his head to the light. She'd only had a few sips of her drink, but he'd downed a whole damn glass of the stuff.

Mark was checking the concealed scabbard in his boot for the one weapon Sonnegut had missed.

"It's there. They didn't find it," she assured him. "I checked for bugs already. The room's not wired unless they have some really sophisticated equipment."

She sat back on her heels and waited, looking around again for any means of escape. Though what she'd do if she accomplished that remained a mystery.

An outright confrontation would be counterproductive. It would blow the whole operation right out of the water. Deborah wanted them confined here for some reason and Renee figured they'd have to stay until someone saw fit to inform them what that reason was.

"If they wanted us dead, we would be," she muttered, more or less to herself. Mark probably wasn't lucid enough yet to listen. "Why put us out of commission? Maybe she just wants to be sure we won't split before you get us in and I set the charges."

Renee smelled coffee. She got up and went into the adjoining bathroom and found the coffeemaker. Someone had also put a selection of pastries there beside it. She poured a cup for herself and one for Mark.

If they had drugged this, too, she would taste it. The drinks they'd been given were purposely unfamiliar so they wouldn't notice an additive. Stupid mistake. Made her feel like a novice, for sure.

But what if they had suspected and refused to drink them? Would Deborah have forced them into this gilded prison at gunpoint?

"Coffee?" Mark muttered, holding on to the door frame and reaching for the cup. He slugged it down without stopping, heaved a sigh and rested his forehead against the wall. "Damn."

She poured him another cup. "What's your take? Why are we prisoners?" she asked when he had finished. She bit into a stale, flaky croissant, hoping food and caffeine would banish any residual fuzziness in her brain.

"Apparently they want us temporarily out of the way," he replied. "Or maybe she's merely playing games."

"Could be. She seems to get off on keeping everyone off balance. Like I said, she might just want to keep close tabs until we finish our jobs. Your *out-of-the-way* theory sounds feasible, though. But why?"

The question grew ever more critical as the hours passed. They had a small television to watch. Renee discovered a minifridge that contained cold canned drinks and wrapped sandwiches. "Whatever Deborah has planned for us, she seems inclined to keep our goodwill. That's a positive sign, I guess."

Mark paced like a caged beast, even growling now and then. He seemed somehow wounded though he didn't have a mark on him. She wondered if part of his attitude was a result of what had happened between them.

She wasn't sure what to call it. Lovemaking? Hardly. Not even comfort sex. Nothing comfortable about it, really. It had left her with burning questions of her own. Maybe he had some of those, too. Questions that they had way too much time to consider, but too much going on to really address.

You could definitely call the night before a complication, she knew that much. It had altered whatever camaraderie they had established. He treated her like a stranger now. Except for that warning grasp of his hand just before he'd gone under whatever drug was used on them. That reaching out haunted her. In it, she had felt more than warning. Or maybe it had been the drug messing with her mind.

"Are you still angry with me?" she asked before thinking it through. Now why had she brought it up, knowing it would probably start an argument neither could run away from?

"No, of course not." And he stopped with that.

Men. Renee rolled her eyes.

Mark stopped pacing and glared at her. "What?"

She threw up her hands in frustration. "Never mind."

"Typical female response," he muttered.

The shrew in her almost got loose, but she beat it back. "Okay then, I just wanted to know if I did or said anything that set you off. If so, my bad. I apologize, all right? Now can we put all that behind us so I can think about business for a change?"

His expression changed slowly until he was almost smiling. "For a change? You think about us a lot, do you?"

"Jeez, Mark! There is no *us*. Don't be such a dope! If you want reassurance, I was wowed, okay? You set off fireworks and blew me away. The earth moved. There. Does that make you feel better?"

His jaw slid to one side as he considered, his arms crossed as he stood there raking her with his dark, penetrating gaze. "Marginally," he admitted with a slight nod. "You gave the impression earlier that it rated only a fraction above a sneeze."

Renee burst out laughing. She lay backward on the bed and covered her eyes with her arm. "Oh God, Mark, you drive me so crazy. What do you care how I rated it?"

"I do care," he said simply. When she moved her arm and looked at him, he was wearing that deadpan expression he used so much of the time, the one that allowed no emotion whatsoever to show.

She realized in that moment that this was his shield. Mark's emotions ran deep, very deep. She recalled how he *had* let them show when he'd spoken of his father. His features might be placid as all get out, but the low timber of his voice betrayed his feelings, as did his self-protective stance.

"I care, too," she whispered and did something she knew was not wise. She raised both arms and beckoned him into them. What a risk of rejection. Big one.

For a few seconds he didn't move. Then, to her surprise, he did. He sat down on the edge of the bed and almost reluctantly lowered himself into her waiting embrace.

Neither said a word. They just held each other for the longest time. No sexual overtones, no kissing, nothing but his thumb idly caressing her temple.

Renee relaxed for the first time since they had arrived at Martine's place. She almost drifted off to sleep, barely hearing him when he first spoke. "We have to figure this out."

"Us?"

He smiled. "That, too, but later. The bombing of that building is definitely connected to Lazlo," he said against her ear. "I wasn't going to tell you because I didn't think it would make a difference, but Lazlo owns that property and has offices there."

She moved her head so that her lips were against his ear. "I ought to throttle you for not telling me sooner."

"Trust issues," he murmured. He raised his head and looked into her eyes, his elbows resting on either side of her. "I am learning the value of trust, Renee." Then he lowered his head and kissed her softly on the mouth.

"Not here," she whispered when he released her lips.

He shook his head slowly. "No, not here. But again," he promised. "Once more. Next time with feeling."

Renee smiled up at him and nodded. To hell with the unwritten rules. Life was too damned short, and in their case, maybe shorter than usual.

She had never wanted a real relationship with a man before. Too risky, for her and for the man. Getting involved meant worrying about the other person, arranging for his safety and keeping secrets from him while you did it. Renee had never thought it worth the trouble. Hadn't wanted to take on that monumental responsibility.

But Mark was like no other man she'd ever met. He was worth damn near any trouble she had to go to. Way past worth it.

Eventually they curled up together and watched a televised movie as they waited for Martine to release them from their comfortable cell and let them know what she planned to do next.

"This is probably just a power play," Renee said, leaning back against his chest with his arms encircling her. She caressed the back of his hand, tracing his long agile fingers with hers.

"We could get out, you know," he told her. "Break the paint seal on a window. There's a ledge leading all the way around the building. A drain pipe on the far side. What do you think?"

Renee shook her head. "We could, but what good would it do?"

"Could you, uh, connect with her? See where she is and what she's doing?"

Renee had already thought of it. It was late afternoon and she was feeling drowsy. Maybe it would work. She took the remote control out of his hand and turned off the television. Settling back against his chest, she cleared her mind and let it drift, willing her subconscious to search out and meld with Deborah Martine's.

* * *

Mark held her, felt her relaxing to a near boneless state. He kept his own breathing slow and even so he wouldn't disturb her effort.

It amazed him that she could do this sort of thing. He never would have believed it if he hadn't seen it for himself. It must have to do with transference of energy or receiving signals.

He admitted he didn't even know precisely how television worked. Or a wireless connection, for that matter. He had a general idea, but took the technologies for granted as did most everyone else who used them. A century ago both would have been lumped within the realm of magic. Was this much different?

Her eyes were closed and she seemed to be sleeping peacefully. One hand twitched a bit, then lay still. He felt an unaccountable urge to wake her, drag her back from wherever she might have gone in her mind. But he knew it was essential that she try any and everything to discover what was going on.

He recognized his own feeling of helplessness, as if his hands were tied while he had a knife available that he dared not use. He hated it.

Patience had always proved the most difficult of lessons for him to master, even as a boy. Patience and objectivity. Lazlo had always warned him that a willingness to wait and cold reasoning were necessary attributes for anyone in their profession.

Renee woke with a start. Mark automatically tightened his arms around her for a few seconds, then released her when she attempted to sit up. "Anything?"

She bit her lips together for a minute, then asked him for something cold to drink. Mark immediately got up and fetched a soda from the tiny refrigerator, popping the top and helping himself to a swallow as he approached the bed. "What?" he asked, handing her the drink.

"They're moving ahead with the implosion, Mark. The location for the charges were all they wanted from me and all they needed to get inside were your notes on the security measures."

"They're in?"

She nodded. "Deborah, Trip and Sonny are setting the charges without us."

Chapter 10

Damn! He had given them too much information. Lazlo had told him to impress them, but Mark knew he should have held back in case they decided to act on their own. "Unfortunately we gave them precisely what they needed."

"We should have faked everything, but I *knew* she would have it checked. I needed her trust for the next phase." She shook her head, took a couple of draughts of the Coke, then blew out a harsh sigh, glanced around the room and then looked up at him. "What do we do?"

Mark took her hand and held it between his own. "I guess this means we go for the window ledge and the drain pipe."

She nodded. "Time to get to a phone and call in the troops. We've served our purpose as far as Deborah's concerned," she added, stating the obvious. "I wonder why we're not dead yet."

Mark gave her hand a comforting squeeze before he got up and went over to examine the window again. "Maybe they thought it would be too difficult to dispose of us here. I imagine they plan to move us to some deserted location to kill us, probably after they blow the building. Or perhaps put us inside it."

She huffed. "If we were anywhere within a few blocks of it, we wouldn't *need* to be inside. They've placed the charges in the right locations if they followed the markings, but unless those charges are detonated at very precise intervals, the structure will explode outward, taking a good-sized chunk of Paris along with it."

Mark retrieved his knife and began working on the window. "I need to warn Lazlo immediately to clear everyone out of that building. He's not expecting it to be set to blow using the real thing. How many live assets do you have within the city?" he asked.

"Three operatives, plus a local task force on call. Response time is about a quarter hour. Thirty minutes, max."

"And I have one man outside here now on surveillance."

"So do I," she admitted. "We need to let them both know the situation. The roundup will be a nightmare, but maybe we can at least grab Trip, Sonny and Deborah."

Mark continued to work. Hurriedly he loosened the paint that held the window shut, hoping the outer trim had not been painted the same way. After a half hour's work, he managed to free the paint enough to force the window open.

He climbed over the sill and beckoned to Renee as he stepped onto the ledge. Just as he turned to search for a handhold, his eye caught movement in the alley below and he looked down.

Piers and Etienne stood about twenty feet apart, looking up, pointing what appeared to be AK-47s directly at Mark. Piers smiled and shook his head.

Mark stuck one leg back inside, colliding with Renee who was about to climb out. "Move and let me back in."

"What's wrong?"

He slid back inside and slammed the window shut. "Time to form Plan B."

She peeked out and saw their escape plan was dashed. "Great."

He brushed the paint flakes off his arms, frowning. "Either we find another route or we wait it out and see what happens." He glanced back at the window. "Your man and mine must be watching the wrong side of the building. That's the best case scenario. Worst case, they might have been taken out already."

Renee nodded. "A strong possibility." She looked at the door. "You're supposed to be good with locks."

He nodded. "If I have picks. Haven't seen anything in this suite that would make a substitute, have you?"

"No. I don't think they would be that negligent after going to this much trouble to keep us secured in here. Maybe we're jumping the gun," she said, tapping her lips with her fingers. "We don't know for sure they plan to get rid of us. Or that they plan to blow the building *today*."

"So you want to play this out and see what happens?" he asked with a cough of disbelief. "Simply sit around and wait? Unarmed, without a chance in hell of defending ourselves? What about the people in Lazlo's building, if it does blow?"

Renee pointed to the window with her forefinger, her thumb cocked like a pistol hammer. "Like the bozos out there are giving us a choice?"

He threw up his hands and began to pace again. Trapped. God, he hated this.

"We weren't made," Renee said shaking her head. "If they knew who we are, we would already be dead. They're taking no chances, though. Deborah firmly believes in checks and counterchecks."

Mark saw her point. "So she has you mark the placement, tests that out with someone in the know, then has someone else do the actual deed. Same with my observations on the security, I'd bet. But I can hardly believe Trip as the demolitions man. You're sure it was him?"

Renee nodded vigorously. "Yes! He was the one affixing the charges and knew precisely what he was doing, too. Nothing much to that really. The trick is in the timing of the detonations. I don't know if Deborah or Trip understand that. Or even if they care." She wearily rubbed her forehead. "You're right. Somehow you've got to warn Lazlo. The people in the nearby buildings need to evacuate, too."

"Maybe she won't detonate right away." He looked at his watch. "It's near time for most office workers to go home for the day. Surely they'll wait until an optimum time when everyone's at work. The question is, can we afford to wait around and see if we're to be included in the detonation party?"

"She's a show-off. I think she'll want us there. Why else would she have mentioned it earlier?"

He nodded. "How we react to the drugging and being locked up might be a test of some sort. If so, then I haven't helped matters by trying to escape through the window."

"No, that's okay, I think," Renee argued. "Who can blame us for that? Somebody locks you in, you try to get out and find out why. Wouldn't anyone?" She flopped down on the bed and glared at the ceiling. "The main problem is that we have to get a warning out."

"I'm working on that," he snapped, busy examining the door hinges. The pins could be removed, maybe. It would take some doing. And some time. But it should take a while for Martine and crew to get the building completely wired, too, so that cut down on the rush. "What time is it now?" he asked.

Renee glanced at her watch. "Just after four. We've been in here for about five and a half hours."

"And how long should it take them to wire the building?" he asked. He had already begun to work on the hinges using his knife to pry and loosen the posts.

"I don't know. Thirty-six charges in all. Figure ten minutes each, I guess around six hours. More if they have to conceal what they're doing."

"They'll have gone in as a phone crew or something that will provide a good dodge and allow them to take in the equipment they need," Mark said, cursing as his knife slipped and nicked his thumb. "Get me something to hammer these pins out of the hinges."

She rushed around and found a marble inkstand on the escritoire and took it to him.

He placed it beneath the post and hammered gently. After much wiggling it about and forcing it upward, he finally removed a pin and tossed it to her. "Go dry soap this so it will slide back in easily. I'll work on the other one."

"Brilliant," Renee said, giving him a pat on the shoulder.

He kept his focus on the pin. "Don't jinx it. I'm trying not to picture two more blokes waiting in the corridor out there to see whether I succeed."

A quarter hour later, with Renee assisting, he carefully moved the heavy door, disengaging it completely from the frame and setting it aside.

"There. We won't be able to relock it, but perhaps we'll get by with it."

The hallway was deserted.

"Hurry! We find the phones and our weapons, call this in and wait to see what they plan to do."

"And if that's to kill us?"

"It won't be," she insisted. "I'm almost sure of it. Even if it is, at least we'll be armed and ready. Deborah's declared repeatedly that she wants to observe the destruction. They'll be in a group to do that and I've been counting heavily on taking them en masse. It's critical."

They had reached the front foyer. Renee jerked open the commode beneath the mirror and found their weapons where Sonnegut had stashed them. "Here. Lock and load. Our phones must be somewhere in the salon since they took them from us after we passed out."

After five minutes' fruitless search, Mark cursed and gave up finding their cell phones. "Keep looking," he told Renee. He went over to the old fashioned gilt-encrusted telephone on the lamp table and lifted the receiver. "No dial tone." He followed the cord and found it plugged in. "Either they disconnected it or it was never in service."

They continued searching for their phones, Mark periodically checking his watch and glancing at the door.

He heard the door open and voices in the foyer. "Quick!" he ordered, grabbing Renee's hand and rushing her back to the bedroom. Together they hurriedly reset the door on the hinges and slipped the pins back in place.

"Maybe we should have taken them as they came in," he said, cursing under his breath.

"What about Beguin and the others? They're outside armed with fully automatics. How far do you think we'd get if our guys are already down? We need to play for time."

Time. Mark didn't figure they had much of that. He heard footsteps. "Should we be contented or outraged?"

"Resigned. Outrage won't sit well with Deborah. But contented wouldn't be normal, either. So resigned, a little ticked off. Sound okay?"

"Makes sense." He wriggled out a comfortable place and posed. "Suppose they notice our weapons are missing from where Sonnegut stashed them?"

"Then we play it any way we can. Shh, they're coming."

The key rattled in the lock and the door swung open. Sonnegut appeared, his toothy smile in place. "Ah, how cozy! Deborah wishes you to join us in the salon."

They crawled off the bed. Renee looked grumpy. "What's with the sleeping draught, Sonny?"

He laughed. "Ask madame."

When they entered the salon, only Deborah was waiting. Mark had expected Trip to be there and felt a sharp pang of disappointment when he wasn't.

Deborah had changed from her classy lounge outfit to basic black, but she still wore her usual catlike smile, her large green eyes narrowed. "Everything is in place!"

Renee plopped down on the couch and crossed her arms tightly as she frowned at Deborah. Instead of commenting on Deborah's announcement, she asked, "Why were we drugged?"

Deborah sat forward, her fingers laced together, almost as if in supplication. "Please understand, darling. I have to be extremely careful. You did a marvelous job marking the ideal locations for the explosives, but I thought it wise to have another contractor complete the actual placement. I knew you would strongly object to having someone else finish what you'd begun." She flared her hands and tilted her head. "So…"

Renee put on a serious pout. "Does this mean I only get half pay for the job?"

"No, no!" Deborah assured her, laughing softly. "You have my word, you'll get exactly what's due you. That's only fair."

Renee gave a grudging nod, her disgruntlement still apparent, but less than it had been. Mark thought her acting skills superb. "So, am I through?" she asked. "Should I go now? You've always said all of us could see it happen." Her lips worked as if she were trying to conceal her disappointment, almost to the point of tears. "I chose the perfect place. I like to watch."

"Well then, you shall, by all means." Deborah had sat back in her chair and crossed her long legs. The keen expression on her face belied her relaxed body language.

Mark watched Renee as closely as Deborah and Sonnegut did.

Renee suddenly stopped pouting and actually grinned. She wriggled to the edge of her seat and leaned forward, her eagerness matching Martine's. "As I said earlier, it's perfect. The tenth floor. There's no glass installed yet that might shatter with the blast. I prepared for everything." She paused for a minute, then added, "I even have masks."

"Masks?" Deborah asked, laughing a little, looking puzzled.

Renee nodded, her enthusiasm picking up speed. "Yes, of course. It's bad for you to breathe in all that dust. I told you, I've thought of everything!"

"So you have and I am impressed. How many masks did you get?"

"Seven. Will that be enough?" She asked the question pointedly.

Mark knew she was trying to determine how many would be present for the event, how many they would be faced with apprehending.

"That will be sufficient. Where are these masks of yours?"

Renee stood. "In my apartment. I'll go get them."

"Sit down, darling," Deborah demanded, then softened her expression. "There's no great hurry.

Mark will be happy to fetch them for us, won't you?" She looked to him for his answer. Every time Deborah asked a question, even though she worded it so politely, it emerged as an order.

Mark nodded, wondering where the devil he could dig up masks on short order. Or did Renee actually have them? If so, when had she gotten them and *why?*

Well, for now he needed to keep up the act, at least until everyone was gathered at the observation point. He just hoped no one discovered that he and Renee were armed.

Renee placed a hand on his forearm and gave it a fond squeeze. Her eyes met his as if she were trying to communicate something. He was no mind reader. He'd just have to wing it. "The masks will be in a box in the wardrobe beneath my empty bags. And could you bring the green knapsack that's in there? It has my binoculars."

Mark had no illusions that he'd be allowed to go back to the apartment without company. Company who would check the bags and boxes they found.

Had Martine guessed who they really were and who they were working for? Impossible, he thought. Even with all the Lazlo resources, he hadn't found a thing on Renee. And his own manufactured background was solid as stone.

Sonnegut prodded his shoulder. "I'll be with you."

No surprise there. Mark got up, dropped a kiss on Renee's cheek and left, his mind working the possibilities.

Somehow he must call Lazlo to have someone defuse the explosives. He had his weapon. He'd have to take Sonnegut out the first chance he got, then hurry to join Renee. He didn't doubt she'd try to take the entire gang by herself.

He worried that the explosives might detonate early since they'd been set inexpertly. Lazlo's people working on the underground level of the building, maybe even Lazlo himself, could be buried beneath tons of rubble if the blasts didn't get them first. Mark had never been inside the secret command post, but he imagined it alive with activity at all hours of the day. Then there were the innocent civilians above ground going about their business.

He had to do *something*. And fast.

Renee prayed that Mark would keep his cool and retrieve the masks she'd asked for. They had been ordered and waiting since right after Deborah indicated that there would be fireworks and that she and the others wanted to witness the destruction. Of course, at the time Renee had thought *she*, as the demolitions expert, would be in full charge of detonation.

Not that there was ever to be an actual explosion, but getting them to that point, all in one place, all distracted by the upcoming show, had been her aim. She had planned a way to take all or most of the culprits without firing a shot in case she had to do it herself before backup arrived.

She shifted restlessly on the couch and pointed to the bar. "Anything to drink over there besides our sleeping potion? I can still taste the stuff." She made a face.

Deborah flashed a parody of a smile. Then she beckoned to Beguin who stood just inside the doorway. "Bring us a juice," she ordered. "We wouldn't want to dull our senses with liquor at this point, now would we?"

Renee sighed as if she were disappointed at that and also still a bit upset about being drugged and locked up. "I wish you would tell me what I've done wrong. You no longer trust me, do you?"

"I'm only employing caution, my dear. You've done an excellent job for which you'll be rewarded. I had someone take over the difficult part of actually placing the charges. You should thank me."

Renee rolled her shoulder and scoffed. "The more people you involve in this, the greater the chance of mistakes. Here I thought we were on the same page and you pull out a different book entirely!"

She accepted the capped bottle of juice from Beguin and popped it open. He resumed his post at the door. His hand remained on his weapon all the while.

"I trust no one," Deborah admitted. She looked almost apologetic. "You've given me no reason to doubt you, darling, but I never depend on one person's expertise, especially in an operation this important. You are very young to have the experience necessary to do what I needed doing."

"You said I did well," Renee argued. "You found someone better?"

Deborah settled back in her chair and tapped her long nails on the arms of it. "I already *had* someone. You were the backup. This was planned months before I even met you."

Renee rolled her eyes and took a slug of the juice. Apricot. She hated apricot. "Well, if he screwed up the placement, the building will blow out instead of in. Detonation must be carefully timed. Does he know that? We could be in danger as we watch it happen."

She saw the other woman's flicker of unease. Then it settled into certainty. "He's competent. We'll all go to the vantage point you suggested. That was brilliant planning on your part." Deborah said it as if offering Renee a sop for the distrust.

"Thank you," Renee snapped. "So will you let me do the detonation?"

For a moment, Deborah seemed to consider it. "No, I promised otherwise. John will do it."

"John?" Renee's eyes widened before she could control her response. "Who the devil is *John?* Your expert?"

Deborah nodded. "You'll meet him when we get there."

Renee decided to capitalize on that split second of doubt she'd seen in Deborah's eyes. "There are fewer than twenty companies worldwide that do this sort of thing with any great success. My father's was one of them, as you know. The demolition community is small, Deborah. Tell me who this person is. I probably know him and can tell you whether his rep is any good. If it's in question…" She let the sentence die, hoping Deborah's doubt would expand it.

"John Trip. He has good credentials."

Renee frowned. "Trip? Never heard of him. If he were any good, I would have. Maybe his creds are faked."

Deborah pushed out of her chair and shook her finger at Renee. "This is professional rivalry and I won't have it!"

Renee realized she had gone too far. If she made Deborah mad enough, she might find herself locked up again and unable to do anything to stop this. "I'm sorry. I just want to make sure everything goes well. So what *do* you want me to do?"

Deborah began to pace. "Furnish the masks. And keep your mouth shut about John."

Renee inclined her head in reluctant agreement and finished her juice. She sat with her legs tucked beneath her and leaned on the arm of the couch. "My masks are important, you know. There will be an enormous dust cloud. Remember the pictures of New York during nine-eleven?"

Deborah smiled with approval and sat down again. "It will not be as bad as that. This is only one building of nine floors."

"Yes, but the fallout will engulf us. I chose that windowless unit to avoid flying glass, but there could be debris. We should have flack jackets. If I have time, I could—"

"Kevlar should do and I believe we have that," Deborah said, beckoning to Beguin. "See Piers. Have him collect some vests."

Renee wondered if she could get any more information about the number of people going without angering Deborah again.

"Well, I know why *I* want to watch," she said with a mirthless laugh. "A little touch of pyromania, I think, or whatever the explosives equivalent of that might be. I love to see things come down in a heap or blow sky-high." She smiled at Deborah as if everything was forgiven. "Tell me, what excites you about it?" Her voice was conversational, just two pals trading foibles.

Deborah got a faraway look in her eyes, a mix of regret and determination. Her heavily ringed fingers twisted the fringed belt she wore into knots.

She spoke through gritted teeth. "Someone needs destroying and from here on, I need to witness every step of his destruction. Until now, I have had to hear about his troubles secondhand."

Lazlo? "So he'll be there when you do it?"

Deborah shook her head. "No."

"Ah, you're going for his property. You plan to hit him in the bank, right?"

"And in the heart," Deborah said, her voice almost crooning. "He will lose more than stone and mortar today. And he will feel responsible, as well he should."

This answered so many questions. Deborah was definitely in charge of this operation. She had hired Sonny and his crew to assist. And she had almost certainly hired John Trip. For what, though? Any fool could figure how to lay a charge. Deborah could have hired a real demolitions expert and probably for a lot less. Mark had said Trip was an assassin by trade, a very expensive assassin.

Uh-oh. The light dawned. Once the mission was complete, Deborah would need to get rid of everyone who could incriminate her if they were apprehended. Or anyone who might decide to blackmail her later. Good ol' John was hired to take care of that with his three bullets to each head and a short stack of business cards.

He would show up at the vantage point to view the implosion. That would give him the opportunity to put faces with names for later hits. And it would give him the advantage of establishing enough trust to get close to his marks. He wouldn't kill them there at the scene. It would be too difficult to shoot that many people at once without being overpowered. He would be waiting elsewhere to take them out, one or two at the time.

This added threat made it imperative that her plan work. She wanted everyone taken alive if possible. If only she had confided the details to Mark. Now she wouldn't have that opportunity.

Deborah was on her cell phone, talking softly in

Italian. Who could that be? Trip maybe? Or some other wild card? Damn, this was not going well.

Renee listened, trying not to appear interested in Deborah's end of the conversation. *"Non potete. Sia paziente. La volta prossima... Sì, naturalmente. Arrivederci."*

Whoever Deborah was talking to would have to hold his horses until the next time.

Renee almost sighed aloud with relief. One less to worry about today, anyway. Was this another of Lazlo's enemies? Deborah's tone and message were a little too firm to be talking to a boss. However it bothered Renee that someone else was out there, privy to this plan, who would get away.

Deborah made another call, this one in French, to Sonny. When she rang off, she faced Renee. "Everyone's ready to meet now. Come with me."

"Now?" Renee demanded, her voice a full octave higher than normal. Too soon! "But Mark's not back with the masks."

"Now."

Deborah plucked a soft wool jacket off the back of a chair near the door and pulled it on. Renee's leather one was in the foyer, folded on top of the commode where her weapon had been stashed. She grabbed it on the way out. Deborah didn't spare her a glance. She either didn't know the gun had been there, or she didn't care whether Renee was armed. She seemed totally focused on seeing that building go down.

Etienne was waiting behind the wheel of a black

BMW, its engine running. Beguin held the back door open for Deborah and Renee, then hopped in front on the passenger side. In horribly nasal French, he turned and informed Deborah that Piers would meet them with the requested vests.

"What about Sonny and Mark?" Renee asked Deborah.

"They will be there, too," she said, giving Renee's hand an absent pat. "Everyone will. Sonny said Alexander knows the location of our viewing."

"Yes, he knows where it is." The car zipped down the side streets and out into heavy traffic. It was after five o'clock. Renee shuddered to think what would happen if things went according to Deborah's plans. So far, it looked good for her. Especially if Mark didn't show up with the masks. Or if he did and the masks didn't work.

Chapter 11

Mark lifted the heavy cardboard box out of the wardrobe and set it on the floor. It had already been opened. Sonnegut flipped open a flap and reached inside. "Gas masks."

"Full face with air purifying filters," Mark noted. "Renee leaves nothing to chance." He couldn't believe his relief at finding them here. Sonnegut had made Mark drive and had kept his weapon in hand the whole way.

Other boxes were stacked beneath this one, but Mark didn't explore. God only knew what else Renee had stored in there. He quickly grabbed the green knapsack she had asked for and closed the armoire doors.

"What's inside that?" As soon as Mark brought it out, Sonnegut snatched the knapsack out of his hands and plundered through it, dragging out each article. "Binoculars. We can use those. Duct tape. Ah, power bars. And a box of condoms?" He giggled and stuffed them back inside. "You are right, my friend. She thinks of everything!" He shoved the knapsack at Mark, still laughing.

They were both on their knees, the box of masks between them. Mark began edging to one side, waiting for a chance to jump Sonnegut. He had no choice but to get rid of this guy. Lazlo had to be warned. He moved a bit closer, pretending to count the masks in the box.

Sonny held up a mask and examined it. "Wonder if the vision is good in these things. Deborah will want to see everything clearly."

He used both hands, taking the one off the pistol at his belt, to tug the mask on over his head. He wriggled it around.

Mark sprang and tackled him to the floor. For five seconds or so, Sonnegut struggled wildly. Then he simply gave up and collapsed, his arms dropping away to either side like dead weights.

A trick? Mark peered into the plastic visor of the mask Sonnegut wore and saw his eyes were closed. He was limp as an overdone noodle.

Mark laughed out loud. Renee, bless her, planned to disable the entire crew at once. He might have gone down with the rest of them since she hadn't warned him the masks were rigged.

He faced the problem of showing up at the vantage point without Sonnegut, but that was unavoidable.

Quickly he rolled the unconscious man over and bound him with silver duct tape from the green rucksack. "Yes, Sonny boy, my clever little Renee thinks of everything!"

He made the call to Lazlo on Renee's landline. "The charges are set, Corbett. Repeat, you have *live* charges in place. Get everyone out now, surrounding buildings, too. And send backup to the one under construction, three blocks north of yours, tenth floor. Get the GIGNs if possible." The Gendarmarie's version of SWAT should do the trick.

"Done," Lazlo snapped and clicked off.

Mark hadn't explained why there were not dummy charges or why the operation had progressed so quickly and to the point of planting anything at all. Lazlo didn't waste breath demanding an explanation. But hopefully now someone was in that building disconnecting wires.

Mark wrestled off Sonnegut's mask and tossed it into the box, then carried it down to the car. The phone call on the way over had been from Deborah instructing Sonnegut to go directly to the vantage point. This was going down *today*. It made sense. They couldn't risk leaving the explosives in place for very long or they might be discovered.

This was unlike any mission Mark had ever had.

Generally he did rescues, one on one. Occasionally he was assigned to infiltrate a group and gather information but he would disappear before the takedown. He never worked with a partner. He never took credit.

But this op, Renee had provided the only useful information he'd been able to get. Her people hadn't been notified of the current situation but Mark had no clue whom to call for her. Renee had become important to him during the past few days. Personally important. Invaluable. It would be a definite hindrance, but her survival outweighed anything, he realized. Even catching or killing Trip.

He parked behind the building under construction. There were no workers visible at this hour. Someone had seen to that, he was sure. He got out of the car and entered through a back door, hefting the box of masks, Renee's knapsack slung over one shoulder.

No security at all, he noted. He entered the service elevator and rode smoothly up to the tenth floor.

Renee had been inside to evaluate the place the day they had scoped out the target, but he had remained outside. She should have given more details about her plan.

Plastic tarps, open steel beams and general construction litter greeted him. The outer walls were finished except for the installation of glass. The inner space was probably destined for those half-walled partitions so common in offices. Mark heard voices in the distance.

He stepped carefully to avoid tripping over the clutter left by the workmen.

"Ah, there you are!" exclaimed Deborah. She pranced forward and looked around him. "Where is Sonny?"

"Guarding the back door. He swore we were followed, but I didn't see anyone. He said we can't be too careful."

She chewed her full lower lip and frowned, still staring back the way he'd come as if she expected Sonnegut to appear in the next few moments. She reached in her pocket, probably for her cell phone.

"Here are the masks," he said to distract her. "Sonnegut says the visibility in them might be less than you'd like. You want to check?" He handed her one.

"We're waiting for John. Then we'll proceed." She gestured excitedly toward the open space with its clear view of the target. Again she glanced in the direction of the elevator.

Mark scanned the area for Renee. She stood off to one side in the shadows. When he nodded to her, she gave him a half smile rife with resignation. He walked over to her and handed her the knapsack. "Everything all right?"

She nodded, her gaze now fastened on the box he had brought in. "We can always hope."

Piers passed out the Kevlar vests as Renee knelt and opened the box of masks. She separated the stack carefully, almost as if she were looking for a particular one. Everyone else was busily strapping on their protection.

"John! You are late!" Deborah exclaimed, throwing up a hand in greeting.

Slowly Mark cut his gaze to the newcomer. Even though he was prepared and determined not to react in any way to seeing Trip, every nerve in his body went on alert. His breath caught in his throat.

Here was *his* target. At that moment, he didn't care if all of Paris collapsed in a heap. He had Trip. The nine millimeter pressed insistently against his spine. It felt as though it pulsed, eager to act on its own.

God, how he wanted to draw it now. His father's lifeless body leaped to mind, as clear an image as Mark had seen in person that night in their kitchen. He ached to empty his clip into Trip without a pause. All fifteen rounds and screw the rest.

But that would leave Renee at risk, on her own against four. He forced air into his lungs and averted his eyes from Trip, looking instead at Martine. Did she have the detonator?

Renee cleared her throat as if to command attention. Mark risked a quick glance at her and saw her slight frown.

He ducked his head in a short nod, his eyes already back on Trip. He couldn't kill him now for another very good reason—his promise to Lazlo. With Trip dead, they would never know who ordered Mark's father's death.

"What's this?" Trip asked, pointing to the masks.

Renee squatted beside the box. Mark put himself directly between her and Trip. Shielding her was as automatic as breathing.

"Sonny?" she whispered to Mark under her breath as he leaned over.

"Nap," he replied with a wink.

She looked up then and asked aloud, "Where's Etienne?"

"With the car. We won't need him," Deborah declared. "Or Sonny, either. John, you have the detonator? Give it to me." She made a gimme motion with her free hand. In the other, she held the mask Mark had given her to distract her from making a call to Sonny.

Trip's face contorted into an evil grin as he handed her a remote control device that was a bit larger than a garage-door opener.

"Wait! Not yet!" Renee exclaimed, jumping up. "We need to put these on first and make sure they're working."

"Clear the visors. See how well you can breathe in them," Mark suggested, motioning to the one Deborah was holding.

Trip's eye caught Mark's then. "Do I know you?"

Mark shook his head and took the mask Renee gave him. He offered it to Trip. "Need some help fitting this?"

"I can manage," Trip said, still perusing Mark's face and frowning.

Mark knew why. He was the spitting image of his

father except for the small beard and moustache his dad had always worn. Mark hadn't worried that Trip might remember the face of one of his victims. There had been so many in the interim.

He ignored Renee's harsh squeeze to his arm as he watched Trip dragging the mask over his head. It covered him to the shoulders. He peered through the transparent visor and shifted the filter with one hand to fit it properly.

Die, Darth Vader, Mark thought, giving him a thumbs-up.

Renee was tugging Beguin's down over his head while the bugger's hands wandered dangerously close to her breasts. Piers was pulling his into place. Deborah was too busy examining the remote detonation device, glancing out the open window and smiling. Mark scooped one of the last ones out of the box. "Better suit up, madame."

"Madame?" she asked with a wild laugh. "My aren't we formal?" She raised her mask, but couldn't don it while holding the remote.

"Here, I'll hold that for you," Mark said with a smile.

"Not on your life. You put the mask on me."

Renee had joined them and she didn't look happy.

"What?" Mark asked her.

"Trip's is *damaged*," she said, a frantic note in her voice catching his attention.

But Deborah was looking over Renee's shoulder. Her body tensed. "What's wrong with them?"

Beguin and Piers were staggering. They crumpled at nearly the same time. Deborah kicked Renee in the knee and ran. Renee fell, rolled and came up, gun in hand.

Mark had his weapon out, his focus whipping to Trip as the man ripped off his mask with one hand and aimed his nine millimeter with the other. He hadn't gone down.

"Duck!" Renee screamed. Mark dived forward. Renee popped off three rounds and Trip grabbed his chest, a look of shock on his saturnine features. His weapon tumbled to the floor as his knees buckled.

"Secure them!" Renee cried as she ran after Martine. "Restraints in the condom box! You have five minutes before they come around. I'll get *her*."

Mark followed her command, though it was all he could do not to dash after her and drag her back. She could be killed. But if he didn't restrain these men, he'd have more gunfire than both he and Renee together could deal with. He had no choice but to trust she could handle Martine.

He checked Trip for a pulse and found one, but he wasn't going anywhere in his condition. Two to the chest and one to the abdomen. If he'd worn a vest like the others, he would still be a threat. Mark bound his wrists with tape anyway. Then he quickly secured Beguin and Piers, leaving their masks on, hoping the residual of whatever knocked them out would keep them that way for longer than five minutes.

He fished a cell phone out of Piers's pocket and punched in Lazlo's number. "It's going down. Now! Detonator is not secure. Repeat, not secure."

Without waiting for an answer, he started after Renee and Deborah. The entire floor was silent. He chose the stairs.

He heard shots before he reached the next floor. Too many shots for two weapons. It sounded like a war zone.

Renee ducked behind a steel toolbox and reloaded. She should have guessed Deborah would have yet another crew stationed as backup. The witch never left anything to chance, damn her.

Who were these guys? She counted at least five shooters besides Deborah. The target hadn't blown yet or they would have felt the shock. Maybe the detonator was faulty. Renee prayed it was, but that building was the least of her problems. She was pinned and bullets were flying. It was only a matter of time till she took a ricochet if one didn't make a direct hit.

Suddenly another shooter burst out of the stairwell. He landed behind a beam very near her. "You hit?" he shouted. *Mark.*

"No." The reports and echoes were deafening, the smell of cordite thicker than an indoor shooting range. Hell, this *was* an indoor shooting range and she was one of the targets.

"Catch!" he ordered and slid a cell phone across

the floor between them. A bullet zinged, missing her hand by an inch as she grabbed the phone.

She quickly punched in control. "Backup, please! We've got five shooters on the ninth floor. Two of us pinned. Ammo's low."

Mark dived across the space between them, slid next to her and fired off three rounds. The return fire was less. "Only two left. One at our three o'clock, one at our six."

"We got three of them?" Renee couldn't believe that. She had mostly been firing blind.

"There must be another way down. These two are covering the escape." His free hand rested on her shoulder, warm and comforting, a partner's reassurance. "You all right?"

"Fine. Let's draw them out." She tried to wriggle from her position between him and the steel box, but his fingers tightened and held her where she was.

"Stay down."

They heard a scurrying sound and in a few moments, footsteps clattering. The sound receded. "More stairs on the opposite side of the building."

He fired again. Nothing. "Well, I guess that's that. We can't give chase. I'm down to a couple of rounds. You?"

"Three," she admitted. "I guess the detonator didn't work, thank God. Maybe Trip wired it wrong. Let's go back up and make certain we don't lose the others. Is he dead?"

"Not when I left, but unless he gets to surgery

soon, he hasn't a prayer." Mark's chuckle was bitter. "Not that anyone sane would actually *pray* for him."

Renee cursed under her breath. "I'm sorry, Mark, but he was aiming right at you. I had to fire."

"Then I should say thanks, shouldn't I? You have Sonnegut. He's bound and gagged in your flat."

She shrugged off the arm he had thrown across her shoulders. "Then I guess *your* mission's complete."

He smiled. "And now I'll go away? Is that what you want?"

"That's what you *do,* isn't it? Set up the take-down, then disappear?"

"Who told you that?" How could she know?

"No one had to tell me. If you ever hung around for pats on the back, your name would be out there as one of us, at least in the inner circles. My guess is you're Lazlo's secret weapon, never surfacing, maintaining the rep he created for you, right?" She blew out a sigh. "Never mind. I don't expect an answer."

She wouldn't get one, either, not that she needed it. His silence on the matter was as good as an admission.

He let the matter drop as they reached their captives and found them stirring. Piers and Beguin had rolled back to back and were attempting to free each other's restraints. Mark kicked them apart, aborting the move. "You're not going anywhere but into custody, so give it up."

"I know you," Trip growled, conscious now, though blood seeped from the corner of his mouth.

Lung shot, Mark figured, feeling no sympathy whatsoever.

"No, we've never met," Mark told him. "You knew someone who looked like me. You shot him in cold blood and left your calling card in his pocket."

There were dozens to choose from, but Mark saw a light dawn in Trip's dark eyes. "Brevet? Ah, yes, you must be...the pup I missed." Trip bared his teeth in a taunting grin. "Looked for you."

"Now you found me." Mark restrained the urge to kick those teeth down his throat. "Who hired you for that job, Trip?"

"Die before I tell," Trip said with a laugh that ended in a cough and a gurgle. He closed his eyes and struggled for breath.

Mark growled a curse. He felt Renee's hand grasp his wrist, the one in which he held his weapon. Well, he did have it pointed at Trip's head. He lowered it to his side and she let go.

They turned at the sound of pounding feet.

Police! Rendez vos armes. Placez vos mains derrière vos têtes!

A bevy of locals wearing SWAT gear surrounded them. Mark laid his pistol on the floor, safely away from the men in restraints. Renee did likewise, shouting in French as she did so, identifying herself and the men on the floor.

Mark knew he and Renee would be hauled in for questioning, along with the others, until their identity was verified. Neither of them carried any

ID for obvious reasons. This was a new experience for him. As Renee had guessed, he usually vanished by this stage of the game.

"This one's an assassin wanted in several countries," Mark declared, pointing at Trip. "Guard him well."

One of the team squatted and felt Trip's neck. "No need for that," he said and stood.

Mark cursed foully. His promise to his father and his vow to Lazlo were history. He looked down at the man who had wrecked his life and caused him such loss and overwhelming grief.

The relief he once thought he'd feel at seeing Trip dead didn't materialize. He felt only an all-encompassing sense of failure.

At the station house, Mark gave his full name and that of his employer. Lazlo would have to recognize him publicly as an employee or else leave him to rot in a French jail under suspicion of terrorism.

There would be articles in the news or, barring that, at least reports filed within several agencies. Either way, Mark would get no further deep-cover assignments.

The problem was, Mark couldn't think of anything else he knew to do with himself. Desk work? Hardly. Regular fieldwork, perhaps.

What if he simply quit altogether, purchased an isolated farm somewhere and grew vegetables? The thought was tempting. He was so damned weary of the kill-or-be-killed lifestyle, anything sounded like an improvement.

Renee argued with the tactical officer in charge even as they were led cuffed toward holding cells. They would be here until their identities were confirmed and their role in the confrontation detailed to satisfaction.

Mark caught her eye and smiled. There was a woman who would never bow to fate. She battled to the bitter finish.

"It will be all right," she assured him. She held up her hands, wrists pressed together with tough plastic bonds. "We'll be out of these in no time."

"I love your optimism," he replied. *I love you.*

That last thought caught him totally by surprise. He wasn't certain it was true. He only knew his yearning for her ran incredibly deep and wasn't limited to the sensation of her body beneath his. *Love, or something very like it.*

She gave him a look that spoke volumes, as if she had actually heard the words. She wore this expression of wonder, or realization. It was almost as if he could hear what she was thinking. *My God, I love you, too.*

Mark smiled at his own foolishness and wishful thinking. He had no precedent for categorizing his feelings for Renee. But the wild fear he experienced when she was threatened, the overpowering need he had to hold her close and the deep satisfaction he felt when she smiled her approval all indicated that she meant much more to him than anyone else ever had. What was between them was surely more than great sex. She was someone he actually knew and respected, not a handy lay he could kiss off and easily forget. Maybe it *was* real love.

The more he thought about it, the more he liked the idea of being in love with her, even though he knew nothing would come of it. Better to have loved and lost and all that, he thought with a wry twist of his lips.

At least he had discovered he was capable of loving.

Chapter 12

Renee heaved a huge sigh of relief when Vanessa Senate and the head of the Paris group, Jack Mercier, arrived, identified her and explained her presence to the police. Mercier was fairly well-known due to a former mission in Paris two years earlier that had involved the local authorities. She exited the holding cell, shook Jack's hand and gave Vanessa a hug. "Am I glad to see you two! Any word on Deborah Martine?"

"Not yet," Mercier said. "They're interrogating the others, but so far nothing. Either the woman inspired a boatload of loyalty or they're scared to death of her."

Renee rolled her eyes. "I'd vote for the fear. I

can't see sexual enthrallment lasting long in stir. So Sonnegut isn't talking? He has to know we've got him dead to rights."

Van shrugged. "I'm sure he's hoping we won't be able to extradite him to the States and he's probably right."

Jack interrupted. "His advocate's already shown up and is in private consultation with him now. After we debrief you, I'll be interrogating him regarding the kidnapping. They *are* allowing us that, so hopefully we'll get the information we need to close our case. We'll petition to have him extradited for shooting the two Secret Service agents, but they want to prosecute him here for his part in the bombing scheme."

"So long as he's put away," Renee said.

Jack nodded. "By the way, the locals found the detonation device, broken as if someone had stomped it. Martine must have ditched it when she thought it didn't work."

"Why didn't it?" Renee asked.

"It did, but not as they expected," Mercier answered. "Apparently Lazlo kept one of his people on site from the outset, watching and waiting to defuse in case charges were ever set. Going by the plans you constructed and that Alexander copied and sent to Lazlo, they located all but an extra one thrown in for good measure. It blew out a few windows on one floor and caused a fire but no structural damage. I figure faulty matériel. Probably old Semtex or whatever they used."

"Whew. Close." Renee had been waiting for a chance to ask the question foremost in her mind. "Speaking of Lazlo, has he arrived yet or sent someone to vouch for Mark Alexander?"

"Your erstwhile *assistant?*" He smiled. "He's gone."

He would be. Renee blinked back the tears that suddenly welled. No. She wouldn't let this get to her. She sucked in a deep breath and straightened her shoulders. So Mark was gone, invisible again until his next assignment. He had never denied that he would fade into the background as he always did. He had never lied to her, she could say that much for him.

And what had she said? *Of course, go on. Vanish. It's what you do.* Why the devil hadn't she asked him to stay, at least stick around until they had a chance to say goodbye?

She could have sworn they had connected earlier. Such a look of love he'd given her, she could almost hear him saying the words. Or maybe she had only wanted to hear them so she'd imagined that. Why hadn't she blurted it out herself? *I love you, you idiot! Don't disappear on me!* Right. As if that would have gone down well, putting him on the spot right there in front of everyone.

Mercier had walked a few steps ahead of them. Vanessa gave her arm a squeeze and shot her a sympathetic look.

"That transparent, huh?" Renee muttered.

"Another assignment's what you need," Van declared.

"Yeah," Renee agreed, rubbing her arms briskly and forcing a smile. "Somewhere warm. I'm freezing."

Van laughed. "Somewhere with crystal-blue surf and hot cabana boys? Dream on, kiddo. You just had Paris, you know. Poor Cate just pulled Seattle. Not exactly prime climate this time of year."

Vanessa ran on, relaying the team gossip Renee had missed the past couple of months. Too soon, they arrived at one of the interrogation rooms where Renee would be required to relate every detail of her mission to Jack and Van.

And then she would fly home, putting an ocean between her and the man she…wanted. She wouldn't use the L word. Shouldn't even have it in her vocabulary. She'd just chalk this up to experience and go on as before. Man, this was hard.

But at least she wouldn't have to worry about him getting caught in the fallout of her future missions. She would have no one to be responsible for but herself. Yeah, right. Instead she would wonder how he was, what he was doing, if he was putting *himself* in danger. Wouldn't it have been infinitely better to stay in touch, to know what he was up to, to exert whatever force she could to make sure he survived?

Okay, she loved him. Might as well admit it. Fat lot of good that did now.

She practically fell into the chair across from Jack and Vanessa. "Okay, let's do this."

"Begin with the warehouse meeting," Jack ordered, clicking on his recorder. "We're up-to-date until then."

If only that hollow place inside her didn't ache so much. She took a deep breath and exhaled. "Maybe I should have gone with my instincts and just shot him to start with."

"Who?" Jack demanded, frowning.

"Mark. I knew he was trouble the minute he walked through the door." She shook her head sharply and sighed.

"Hey, I thought he helped you!" Van exclaimed, leaning forward.

Renee scoffed at herself, dragging her thoughts back to the job at hand. "Oh, with the case, yeah, he did."

Jack cleared his throat. "You want some coffee? Maybe get your head together before we start debriefing?"

She wrinkled her nose and raked a hand through her hair, hating the way it felt. Hating the way *she* felt. "I'm about as together as I'm gonna get today. Just bear with me and let's get on with it."

Cassandra had made it out of the building before all hell broke loose with her second wave of hired guns waiting on the floor below. It paid to plan ahead.

Sonny was missing, had probably run. Etienne

had driven her straight to the metro station where he parked the car and abandoned it. The metro ride back to the city had taken less than twenty minutes. At Etienne's tiny flat, she ditched her Deborah Martine persona for good. She stripped down to her camisole, donned a pair of his jeans, swept her hair beneath a cap and borrowed his weapon. She had to hurry now. There were things she must do herself if she wanted to go home and resume her life as Cassandra DuMont.

Etienne was fumbling in his waist-high refrigerator for something to eat. Cass leveled his nine millimeter and put one round in the back of his head. Then she calmly walked down the stairs and back to the metro, mentally tallying all she had to do next and in what order. Organization was key.

When she exited the station, she walked off the main street, wiped and tossed the weapon deep into an alley where she knew it would soon disappear and incriminate whoever used it next.

She continued on for several blocks, then went in and set a fire that would gut the apartment where she had been living with Sonny. Only one chore remained.

Entering a small shop on the main thoroughfare, she purchased a cheap, prepaid cell phone, made a call to her organization and arranged for someone reliable to get rid of Alexander and that bitch, Renee, in case Trip hadn't managed to do so. Not that they posed a threat to her now—Deborah

Martine was no more—but she simply couldn't abide anyone duping her as they had done.

She wondered about Trip, whether he had accomplished what she'd hired him for, or if he had been killed. No matter. She wouldn't need him again.

She threw the phone into the sewer. Now she must go home. This entire plan had been a fiasco from the outset, a lark turned to carrion.

She should have taken into account how impossible it was to get good help these days, especially in this quarter.

The whole episode had exhausted her, but at least she should be able to sleep soundly tonight in her own bed.

There was always tomorrow. Next time around she would finish Lazlo and be done with it. Perhaps Sonny had been right all along. Simple was better.

Mark walked all the way to the plane with Corbett Lazlo. The small private jet was about to take off for London from a private airport outside Paris.

The police had released Mark after a couple of hours in the cell on the basis of a phone call. He had asked after Renee the moment he was free, but the officer in charge gave him a blank look and no information whatsoever. Not much of a surprise there.

Mark did have another surprise, however. Corbett had been waiting for him in the limousine when he'd come out.

"This woman, Deborah Martine, do you have any idea what she might have against you?" Mark asked him.

"None whatsoever. We have brief footage from a surveillance camera they overlooked. Her face wasn't really clear, but I didn't recognize her as anyone I know." His brow wrinkled slightly and his mouth drew to one side. "At least I don't think…"

"She reminded me of someone, too, but I still can't think who it might be. Maybe she just had that sort of face. Since we've never run in the same circles, I can't see how we could both have known her," Mark said.

Lazlo shrugged. "Perhaps Trip was behind the effort, after all. He did set those charges."

"I'm sorry he was killed, but I don't believe he would have given us a name, Corbett. He actually told me he would die first. And he laughed."

"Yes, well, you did find him. At least your father is partially avenged. And I will get to the bottom of this, Mark," Lazlo said, his mind obviously working on another angle of the investigation.

They had reached the plane. "Well, I'll say goodbye for now, Mark. Scotland Yard is waiting. Inspector Cameron will be ecstatic when he learns you've identified Trip as the man who killed your father. The case has always been his, after all."

"I just wish we could have learned who was behind the contract on my father before Trip died."

Corbett put a hand on his shoulder, a rare occurrence Mark could recall happening only once, the night his father was shot and Lazlo had made their pact.

"Trip was a killer, Mark. He got what he deserved."

"So am I. Maybe you don't see it that way," Mark said. "But I have killed, Corbett, and on your behalf."

"Never in cold blood, but in defense of yourself or others," Corbett argued. "You must know how valuable you are to the organization. To me."

"How valuable I *was*, perhaps. My cover is blown and I'm of no further use." He paused. "I don't *want* to be of further use, Corbett. Let me go."

Lazlo looked him squarely in the eyes, frowning. "You were always free to go, Mark. If you didn't realize that, I'm sorry. Catching Trip seemed to be your only goal in life and I've done everything within my power to support that."

"And I thank you. I do," Mark said simply and stuck out his hand. "Now it's over. I'm done."

"It's time. Your objective has been met. The rest of this puzzle is mine to sort out." Corbett held on to his hand when Mark would have let go. "Watch your back, son." Without another word, he turned on his heel and went to board his waiting jet.

Son. Mark stood there until the runway was bare of everything but a light dusting of snow.

Despite their infrequent meetings, he had

depended on Corbett in a manner of speaking. Now they no longer had that link. Would he actually miss Lazlo? Probably. He shook his head and watched the plane's lights disappear into the clouds.

Mark had severed the last tie to his old life, if he didn't count his Swiss bank account and the empty house in London that he hadn't entered since he was thirteen. He would sell the place and include the ghosts in the bargain, he decided. The money from the sale plus the funds he had accrued would support him for a number of years.

The future lay as a blank slate before him and he found himself with no chalk in his hand. He turned, walked slowly out of the airport and climbed into a taxi.

"Où voulez-vous aller?" the cabdriver asked.

Where, indeed?

"Rue St. Jacques," Mark said. Nothing was left there but memories. However, they were pleasant memories and he felt like clinging to them for a while, just until he got his bearings.

When he reached the apartment building, he trudged up the stairs, realizing now that he had been hoping Renee might have returned here before flying home. He imagined her up there collecting her gear. He wished to the depths of his soul that he could see her once more.

The door stood open and a stranger was carrying a plastic rubbish bag from the kitchen. The young woman startled when she saw him, then smiled. *"Ce qui vous veulent, monsieur?"*

What did he want? Good question. He glanced around the lounge, now tidy, almost sterile. *"Je veux louer l'appartement,"* he said, surprising himself yet again. He had no business renting a walkup in Paris. He had no business in Paris at all. But the idea of living here where he and Renee had been together appealed to him at the moment.

The girl informed him the place was already let and had been for more than a year.

"It's obviously vacant," he argued, no longer bothering with French since her accent was definitely American. A guest worker, perhaps a student supplementing her income. "I happen to know the person who lived here has recently moved. Yesterday, in fact."

She merely shrugged. "It's already rented. I swear."

"Ah." He got it then. Already let, for over a year. English speaking housekeeper. American. This was a safe house, one of the U.S. assets to be kept available. "Never mind, then. I must have the wrong address."

So where did he go now? For a moment he considered going to Deborah Martine's on the off chance the Americans, Renee in particular, might be there, still investigating.

"No, she probably wouldn't," he muttered to himself. He turned and started back down the stairs.

"Hey, if you want to see her that badly, why don't

you ask where she is? Another chance meeting is about as unlikely as winning the lottery and you've already had one big win."

Mark stopped and turned, his hand on the banister, and looked up the seven or eight stairs that separated them.

The girl was grinning, waiting for his response. She raked her dark hair back behind one ear, then propped her free hand on her jean-clad hip. "Well?"

"You're one of them," he said. No question. The girl had read his mind. Or perhaps he was woefully transparent.

She inclined her head. *An admission?* "Try the Claris," she said.

"Thanks. I owe you." He didn't ask her name. He doubted she would give it anyway.

She raised the small sack of rubbish and tossed it at him. "I'm Danielle. Make yourself useful on the way down, Brevet."

When his surprise abated, she had already gone inside the apartment and shut the door. It was the first time in years that anyone had addressed him using his real surname. All his records listed him as Mark Alexander. That lot Renee ran with were unusual. But Renee might have told her.

He hurried down the stairs, ducked into the alley and deposited the trash in the proper container. "Alexander, you are now retired," he quipped as he slammed down the lid and dusted his hands together. "Brevet is reborn."

Mark Brevet. Mark Brevet. The name ran through his mind like a scrolling marquee. *Renee Brevet. Mrs. Renee Brevet.* He laughed out loud, garnering strange looks from a couple of tourists he passed along the way.

"C'est l'amour. Nous fait des imbeciles," he said, laughing when they eyed him warily. He felt the fool, but he didn't care. He was a loving fool.

He reached the bridge and paused to catch his breath and view the cityscape at dusk. The river smelled of fish, the light snow was turning to sleet and a nasal siren singsonged in the distance as it plowed through the evening traffic.

Paris, City of Light. The perfect place to emerge from the darkness, to come in from the cold. He had never liked the city before, but even in icy November it felt like heaven to him now. Renee was still here and he was going to find her.

The shot came out of nowhere, chipping the stone balustrade not four inches from his hand.

Renee jerked fully awake, her heart racing. "Mark?" she cried, scrambling off the bed and grabbing her weapon. She shoved it into her waist-band and snatched up her coat. Cursing her boots, she tugged them on and stomped to settle her feet inside. Then she ran, throwing open the door, taking the stairs two at the time.

She didn't pause to question the vision. Mark was in trouble. He was unarmed and taking fire.

Pont Neuf? She thought, judging by the snippet of landscape she'd seen. Which way had he run? Right Bank. Notre Dame spire to his right. Damn, she had no transport and it was too far to hoof it.

She fished in her pocket and came up with a fifty Euro note, all she had left. Could she find a cab?

No taxis. Where the hell were they? Frantic, she waylaid a cyclist paused at the curb to light a smoke. *"Ici!"* she said, pushing him off the bike as she shoved the bill into his hand. *"Merci!"*

He shouted once in protest, but she didn't stop to explain. She pedaled like Lance Armstrong, dodging cars that honked like a gaggle of angry geese.

Was Mark headed this way? Had he found a place to hide? Renee knew she should stop and try to connect with him. Not much hope of that with her nerves shot and her mind in turmoil. Fear shook her to the core. Someone was trying to kill him and he had no defense. They would have kept his weapon to check ballistics from the crime scene.

"Mark," she said, grinding the name through gritted teeth and focusing her mind toward his, trying to recall everything she had been encouraged to try when exploring psychic avenues beyond her remote viewing capability.

Connecting psychically had never worked for her before, but she kept thinking of that brief incident when they were being taken into custody. *I love you.* God, she hoped that hadn't been sheer fantasy.

She muttered between her teeth as she pedaled.

"This way, honey. Come *this* way. *Think* about me. Follow the link. C'mon, we can do this." She pumped faster, hopping onto the sidewalk to round a minibus. "Café Rouge," she said aloud, fixing it firmly in her mind. It was on the way. He knew it well. *Brunch with Deborah and Sonny, remember? Go there, Mark. Go there!*

Her breath heaved painfully as she leaned forward over the handlebars. The bike was no ten-speed, but she put the thing in the highest gear she could. Her thighs ached. Her calves screamed.

Two blocks. One. There. She tossed the bike against the side of the building and dashed inside, shoving chairs aside as she hurried to the little courtyard out back. Would he be here? And if he was, would he risk hiding in a no-escape zone like that? There was a high stone wall around it. Wall. The word refused to exit her mind and allow an alternative to form.

She went with it. Gun in hand, she burst through the doorway and dropped to a firing stance. The courtyard was empty, tables wet, dim light glancing off the surfaces.

"Mark! You there?" she called out and a movement caught her eye.

"What took you so long?" he asked, peering over the edge of the thick stone wall. Then he slid off the top and landed on his feet with a bounce. He closed the space between them in three strides, grabbed her and kissed her within an inch of her life. She melted into him, greedy for reassurance, needing to seal their connection.

"I knew you'd come," he gasped, his voice gruff with feeling. "I called to you with my mind. Don't know what made me think of doing that. But somehow I knew you'd hear." Then he put a bit of distance between them and frowned down at her. "I've drawn you into danger and that was never my intent."

"You needed me. I'd call if I needed you, count on that!" Renee shrugged and glanced nervously at the door she'd left open. "Did you lose the shooter?"

He made a rueful sound and shook his head. "I used every evasive tactic known to man, but who knows?"

"Did you see him?"

"No."

"It could be either Deborah or Etienne." Renee patted her coat pockets. "Do you have a phone? We need to call for a pickup."

"No phone. No weapon," he admitted. He seemed troubled.

"Are you all right, Mark?" She brushed a hand over his brow.

"Yeah, I think." He shook his head and ran a hand through his hair. "I quit today."

She couldn't believe it. "You quit?" That jogged another idea. "What if Lazlo uses a permanent severance plan? Could he have sent someone after you?"

"No! That's ridiculous. It's not Lazlo."

Suddenly he strode back over to the wall. "Let's

get out of here. I'll give you a boost." He made a stirrup with his hands.

Renee didn't argue. She was too busy thinking.

Up and over the wall and down the back alleys they went. She led him to the hotel Claris where she knew he would be safe.

"Oh, no, you're not leaving," she declared after he had seen her to the door of her room. She locked her fingers around his wrist.

He kissed her lightly on the mouth. "I'll see you again, Renee. You can count on it."

"Are you nuts?" she said, dropping her voice to a whisper since they were still in the hall. With her free hand, she opened her door and virtually dragged him inside, shutting the door behind them. "You don't have a gun. You don't have a phone. You don't even have a warm coat! Do you seriously think I'll let you back out on the street like that?"

He smiled and raked her windblown hair out of her eyes. "I'll become a ghost until I'm outfitted, I promise."

She coughed a bitter laugh. "You'll become a ghost for real if you get shot!"

Chapter 13

A firm knock on the door interrupted the argument. "Who is it?" Renee called.

"It's Jack. What's going on in there?"

She jerked the door wide and flailed an invitation with one hand. "Come on in and explain the facts of life to this half-witted Brit! He thinks he's James Bond."

Mercier raised one eyebrow. "Double-0-eight?"

"He's on somebody's hit list and now he wants to go crawling around the city to find out who and why."

"Sounds reasonable to me," Mercier said. "I'd want to know, wouldn't you? Probably this Martine person."

She bit her lip to keep it from trembling and

looked helplessly from one man to the other. For goodness' sake, she couldn't cry! Not in front of Mark and certainly not with her boss looking on.

Renee sucked it up and pounded a fist in her palm. "Okay, here's what we do," she said. "We call Lazlo, rule him out or zero in. Get a mind read on him. Can Vinland get it over the phone?"

Mercier nodded. "He could, but he's in Thailand at the moment and I expect he's fairly busy. You think Lazlo's behind it? Why?"

"Mark quit. Lazlo's a huge long-shot, I know, but Mark does know where all the bodies are buried. So who else can do it?" she demanded, ignoring Jack's questions. "Cate?"

"Not available."

Mark spoke up then. "This is ridiculous. Lazlo wouldn't kill me. Just loan me a weapon if you feel moved to help. Otherwise, I need to go now so I can…appropriate one."

"See? He'll be forced to steal! And heaven only knows what else! Jack, get someone to do what I ask. Please."

"What about your friend at the safe house?" Mark suggested.

"Dani?" Renee asked frowning. "She's no reader."

"She read me a while ago, knew I was out to find you and even called me by my real name."

Jack held up a finger to interrupt and turned to Renee. "You do this," he said thoughtfully. "You can, you know."

She rolled her eyes and threw up her hands, but she was up against the wall here. Well, she could *try.* "Fine." She marched over to the nightstand and snatched up the phone. She glared at Mark. "I need a number."

He gave it. Reluctantly and with another assurance that Lazlo was not involved. Angrily she punched in the number and waited.

Lazlo answered on the third ring. "Yes?"

"Corbett Lazlo?"

"Who's this?"

"Renee Leblanc. Someone just attempted to kill Mark Alexander. Do you know anything about that?"

"God, is he all right? Where is he?"

Renee sensed real concern, heard the worry and affection when Lazlo spoke Mark's name. "He's alive."

"In hospital? Which one? I'll be there within two hours. Less, if possible. Tell him I'm on the way."

Renee concentrated, but all that was working was her plain old intuition. That rarely failed her, though, so she went with it.

"He's not injured. Do you know anyone who might want him dead?"

There was a definite pause.

"Mr. Lazlo?" she prompted.

"Several of my people have been killed recently, as you know, Agent Leblanc. This attempt on Mark's life might be a part of that."

"Then we should ask ourselves who knows that Mark was one of yours, shouldn't we?"

"Believe me, I *will* find out," Lazlo promised. "In the meanwhile, tell him to disappear, to keep safe. Assure him that he's done his part, that he *must* let me handle the rest. This is an order, my last order for him unless he wishes to come back when this is settled. Would you tell him that for me? Convince him to do it?"

"Oh, you can count on that. And good luck, sir." She clicked off and put down the handset.

"It's not Lazlo," she said. "He insists that you vanish until he can determine who's behind this. He's commanded you to do this for your own good. When it's over, you can return, but not before, and then only if you want to work for him again."

"You'll come with us, of course," Mercier added. "After all you did to help Renee with our mission, the least we can do is provide you security. Do you have a passport?"

"Wait a second! I'm not running away. I want this settled!" Mark argued.

Renee looked at Mercier. "Sir, would you excuse us? I have some convincing to do here that you don't need to be a party to."

Mercier shot Mark a rueful look. "I'll just go and see about transportation…or something." He left.

Renee turned on Mark and shook a finger under his nose. "You *are* coming with us if I have to use the rest of that duct tape."

Mark smiled down at her and took her hands in his, threading their fingers. "Tempting as hell, but you know I can't, Renee."

"Why not? Are you itching to kill someone else or give them another chance at you? What does it take to get you out of this business you hate? A body bag?"

"Who says I hate it?" he demanded, letting go of her hands and turning away from her. "Who do you think you are, trying to tell me what I should do?"

"Just the one who *loves* you, stupid! Probably the *only* one since you're such a pigheaded fool with a death wish!"

Mark threw back his head and laughed. "This is unreal. *So* unreal."

She stepped close behind him. "Turn around and kiss me, Mark. *That* will be real, I promise."

Slowly he turned and looked down at her. She raised her lips to his and melted against him. She joined her hands to his and slid her arms around his waist. The kiss went wild in a heartbeat. His mouth grasped hers, devoured, plundered as if searching for the source of life. She kissed him back, deeply, sensuously, holding on to her own wits by a very slender thread while trying her dead level best to steal his.

Until suddenly he realized his wrists were bound behind him and jerked his mouth from hers.

"Damn you, Renee." He ground out the words, his lips only inches from hers. She could feel his suspicion flare. God, he thought *she* was the one who wanted him dead?

The paranoid ingrate. She'd just told him she loved him, but he hadn't even seemed to notice that. "Will you go calmly or do I have to drug you?" she asked, her expression deadpan. But he didn't get the joke. He really wondered if she was the one who was after him.

He just looked at her, as if his heart might break. He wasn't fighting to get free. He just stood there.

"I don't want you to die, Mark," she whispered. "I think it would kill me if you let that happen."

He didn't move.

Slowly she took a small Swiss army knife from her pocket, walked around behind him and snipped the slender bonds she had used. "Okay then, it's your choice. Take up the old job you never liked anyway...or come with me." She smiled sadly. "*Be* with me."

"You say you love me. It's the shared danger, our necessary proximity, as you once said, the—"

"Mind-blowing sex. Yes, all that, too, but I *care* about you, Mark, and need you, want to be with you. I love you. Really."

"You can't possibly *love* me, Renee." He sounded almost as if he was trying to convince himself more than her. He chafed his wrists, rubbing them much harder than was necessary.

Jeez, he had been bound for less than a minute, not long enough to interrupt circulation. Nerves, she decided. She made him nervous.

"I admit you make it nearly impossible some-times," she said honestly. "But I'm afraid I do."

"You don't even know me," he argued, but she could see the hope in his eyes. The want to believe. Did he let her see it or was his guard simply down?

She brushed a hand over his cheek and with her thumb touched his mouth, that wonderfully mobile mouth that did more to signify his thoughts than his eyes. It tightened with determination, probably to set her free or some such nonsense.

"I don't do friendships," he stated categorically. "Never have."

"Never?" she asked, sliding her hands around his neck and toying with his nape. "I thought we had gotten at least that far."

He cleared his throat and looked away, not meeting her eyes, but he didn't pull away from her. "Long ago, when I was a boy, I guess I did. But not after…" He took a deep breath. "This…what I feel for you, could be the isolation catching up to me." He was fighting for excuses.

"Then let's explore it," she offered, perfectly willing to give him time to come to the same con-clusion she had reached. "After your father was killed, you knew anyone you remained close to would be at risk, or maybe put you at risk, from John Trip. Lazlo convinced you of that, didn't he?"

"And he was right. I accepted that."

She nodded, in full agreement. "And you cut all ties. But Trip's gone now, Mark. The object of all that hatred is no more. You're free to be who you are, who you were meant to be."

When he met her gaze, his was full of regret. His voice dropped to a whisper. "I'm not sure I know how. I said you don't know me, but the truth is, I don't even know myself. I became someone else then, a creature bent on revenge. Every move I've made since the age of thirteen was directed toward that. Somehow, I knew I would be different when it was over. And I am," he admitted as he embraced her tentatively. "But I always thought I would feel…I don't know, better maybe. Now there's just this empty space where the need for vengeance lived."

She looked up at him, holding his dark eyes with hers. "I'll help fill it, Mark, if you let me."

He kissed her softly and threaded his hands through her hair, regret heavy in his eyes. "I have to say no. I have to finish this no matter what Lazlo says."

She thought for a minute, then stood away, her hands on her hips. "Okay. We'll do it your way. Where do you want to start?"

His smile was a little condescending, she thought, or maybe just tender. "You can't," he told her. "You'll go back to Virginia, to your job and your friends. I have to do this alone."

"Nope!" she said, grinning with enthusiasm. "Either you let me come with you or I'll track you. If you insist on going ahead with it, you're not doing it by yourself."

His eyes rolled as he scoffed. "That's black-mail, Renee."

"Yes, well, it carries less of a sentence than kid-napping, you gotta admit."

Now she'd made him angry. His jaw clenched along with his fists and those great lips of his were a straight line.

"You know I'll get you one way or the other," she warned him with a lift of her left eyebrow. "See, I know your secret. You *want* to be got."

Chapter 14

Mark settled into the apartment Mercier had procured for him. On the flight over the day before, he had held on to his anger toward Renee, knowing all the while she was gloating over her successful coercion.

Every time she had looked at him, she wore a sly smile he wanted to kiss off her face. But she hadn't said another word about *them*. She hadn't initiated any conversation or tried in any way to persuade him they could be together.

Maybe she thought he had objected to the trip because he wanted to get away from her. That worry bothered him more and more as his anger wore thin. Of course, she cared about him or she wouldn't have gone to such great lengths to make him leave France. Forced him, really.

Now here he was in a strange flat in a strange city in a strange country trying to think what he would do with himself. His weeks at the nearby training facility two years ago had left little time to become acquainted with anything outside of it. If he was to be here for any length of time, he really should scope out the landscape.

He put on sweats and trainers, intending to get the lay of the neighborhood. It had been dark and foggy when Mercier drove him here and he had only a vague idea of the surrounding area. He'd slept most of the day, catching up on the lack of sleep during the op. The late afternoon sun beckoned him outdoors.

The doorbell chimed. He tensed immediately, then realized he had no reason to reach for his weapon. Mercier had said he would stop by today or send someone to see how things were going. Mark didn't even hope it would be Renee. He was certain she was leaving the next move up to him.

Mark strode over and opened the door without even checking the peephole. He'd never done that before. It was an excellent way to get shot in the head.

It *was* her. "Hi," she said, wearing a bright expression that seemed a bit false. "Want to go for a beer? Some of the guys…" She waved her hand in the direction of the street. "Well, we don't want you to feel abandoned or anything. I…*we* know you don't have any friends here yet."

"Or anywhere else," he answered wryly, embarrassed by the admission he had already made to her. "But you don't have to become my minder, Renee. I'm perfectly capable of—"

She pushed past him into his new lounge. *Living room*, he reminded himself. Had to get in tune if he was to live here for a while.

"Goodness, early Holiday Inn! We have got to do something with this place, Mark. Or get you an unfurnished and make it a little more homey. This is downright cold."

He would have said utilitarian. Basic necessities. All that he needed. But it wasn't all he needed and they both knew that.

Without pausing, she marched down the short hallway and into the bedroom. "*Hmph*, no mint on the pillow. There's a surprise."

She reached into the tote bag she carried and brought out a bottle. "Here's wine. That should help you endure in the meantime."

"I thought we were to go for a pint…a beer," he reminded her as he accepted the bottle. "With your guys."

She glanced at her watch. "Meeting them at Christa's in about an hour. That's our favorite watering hole. Thought I'd give you time to get dressed."

"Suit and tie?"

She laughed. "Oh, hell, no! You could go as you are, but I really want to get you out of those sweats."

"Why?" he asked, grinning at her proprietary attitude. And the suggestion of getting him naked.

She cast him a sidewise look. "Wrong color for one thing. Basic black has its charm, but I plan to jazz you up a little in the future."

He couldn't stand it any longer. He tossed the bottle on the bed, snatched her bag out of her hand and lowered it to the floor. "Jazz me, then. You know, of course, the original connotation of that word."

"Jazz?" Her voice was soft, as sensual as the feel of her when he slid his arms around her.

"Look it up," he told her, dragging her closer, caressing her back with his hands, her front with his body. She felt so damn good, a perfect fit.

She raised her mouth to his and whispered, "I don't need a dictionary." She kissed him tentatively, then drew back to look up at him. "What I need is you, Mark. How can I convince you how much I need you? Love you?"

"Good start right here," he told her, backing her to the bed and laying her down gently. He lay down beside her and nestled his face in the curve of her neck, inhaling her sweetness, loving the scent of her skin, her hair.

"You love me, too, you know," she said with a sigh.

"Do I?" he asked, tickling her ear with his tongue. "You're so sure?"

She made a small sound of pleasure deep in her throat before she answered. "I don't need the words." How eagerly she responded when he cupped her breast, when he slid open the buttons of her shirt. "I don't need promises," she added, nearly breathless. "I don't need a paper or rings or anything. Just time," she said with a conviction Mark couldn't ignore. "Just you."

Mark knew he was lost. Renee had sealed her fate coming to him this way and offering her heart and body so generously. Even if he didn't love her, he wasn't sure he could have refused her. He felt a flood of warmth that had nothing—and yet everything—to do with his arousal. He wanted her more than breath. He loved her more than life. Why not tell her that? Would she believe him now after he had put up so many objections?

No, the words had to mean something, be said at the right time, not uttered in response to hers, or given when he was so clearly caught up in sexual urgency. Instead he kissed her as soulfully as possible and immersed himself in pleasing her as skillfully as he knew how.

He played with her lips, tracing them with his tongue, then finally claimed her mouth, teasing her, drawing away when she would deepen the kiss. She groaned impatiently, fueling his need to give her what she wanted. But he held back, determined that this would be for her, all for her, to show her how he cared.

She fought their clothes, her hands grasping and tugging. He helped, his own movements slow and deliberate, until nothing came between them but a need greater than any he had ever known. Renee was all he wanted and he wanted all of her. Problems knocked at the back of his mind, but he ignored them. They could work everything out. They could.

Suddenly she pushed him away. For a second he thought she had changed her mind, but then she leaned toward him and trailed openmouthed kisses down his neck, raking her fingers through his chest hair and lower, across his belly and down. Her mouth followed and he groaned in near defeat. The little devil was taking charge.

Mark clasped her wandering hands, pushed her to her back and covered her. "Not this time," he rasped. "Later."

He found her breast, firm and ripe and pouting for his kiss. She bowed beneath him, raised her hips in a blatant invitation, then a demand, that he couldn't refuse.

She met his thrust with a wild little cry that blew his intention to make this last. Her legs wrapped his, her arms locked around him like a velvet vise and her teeth raked his shoulder as she gasped.

He tried to hold still, to imprint the blinding sensation of her insistent heat enclosing him. But control slipped. His body took over and pounded into her of its own accord. She cried out, a sound of pleasure so keen and sweet it echoed in his mind. He would hear it forever, that sound. It opened some deep tap within him and every wish, want, and need he had denied poured out of him and into her just as he found release.

Who was he kidding? he thought as he tried to get breath back into his lungs. He could hardly call it a release when she had enslaved him so completely. Renee owned him, body and soul.

God, but it felt so good to belong.

"See?" she whispered, the word a nearly breathless exhale.

"That I do love you?" he asked, nuzzling her neck, feeling the rapid pulse there with his lips. "Absolutely. Got it now."

She hummed, another of those sounds she made that sent a current through his veins. "You over your mad?"

He laughed, palming her firm little behind and giving it a fond squeeze. "I would think so. You plan to rule the roost, don't you?"

She kissed him. "By any means possible. We'll have a wonderful war, won't we?"

"You mean when we're married and fighting for the upper hand?"

"Cor, what sort of backhanded proposal was that, Alexander?" Her English accent was atrocious. And so endearing he had to smile.

"It's Brevet, remember? Since you're going to share it, you might as well get used to it. You'll be Mrs. Mark Alexander Brevet."

"Will I now! And you're so certain I'll agree to be that when you haven't even *asked* me?" Her voice held a grin, though he couldn't see her face. She was nibbling his shoulder.

Mark raised up and looked down into her face. "I love you, Renee. I adore you, admire you and desire you more than any person I have ever known. I don't believe I can live without you. I don't want to try. Will you be my wife?"

She sighed and stretched her arms above her, then rested them loosely on his shoulders. "That's much better."

The fact that she hadn't said yes threw him. "Isn't that what you want, too? Marriage, maybe a family one day? House in the suburbs?"

"How about a dog?" she said, shrugging slightly. "Never had a dog."

He shook her none too gently. "Answer me! Will you marry me or not?"

Her laugh was a little wild as she hugged him to her and planted a kiss on his ear. "Of course I will, you idiot. What else would I do with you?"

Mark released the breath he'd been holding and rolled his eyes heavenward. "Thank God!"

Later, when they had joined the group at Christa's, Renee began to wonder whether Mark had changed his mind. They had agreed to wait about announcing their plans. Everyone would worry they were rushing things. They were, of course.

A long engagement sounded right, she supposed, but she had never been one to hesitate once she made up her mind. Maybe Mark needed more time? If this was to work, she had to learn to compromise.

She looked at Mark. Though he had little to say, he was putting on a friendly front, not easy for a man who had gone it alone for so many years. Vanessa and Clay Senate, Dani and Ben Michaels, and Jacob, the newest member of COMPASS, had made him welcome. The hot roast beef sandwiches, the beer, the ambience of the comfy bar and friends around her warmed Renee, but she was afraid Mark felt uncomfortable.

"We'll leave if you want," she whispered in his ear.

For a long moment, his gaze rested on hers. Then he smiled, for real. "Sorry if I seemed preoccupied. Being here this way just got me thinking of something I need to do." He pushed away from the table. "Would you excuse me for while? I'll be back, but I really have to make a couple of phone calls."

Renee waited until he left the bar. Then she followed him outside. The air was crisp and cold. She breathed it in, hugging herself. Mark was on his cell phone, leaning into a corner of the entryway. She snuggled against him. "Mind?"

He shook his head and surrounded her with one arm. Then he spoke into his phone, obviously excited. "Tomcat? Hi. Mark Brevet here. Sureshot. Remember me?" A huge smile broke out and he hugged Renee to his side. "No, mate, I'm very much alive in spite of what you might have heard. Hell yes, the three musketeers! Of course, I'll tell you everything soon enough and it will curl whatever hair you have left!"

He laughed out loud at whatever his friend replied, then asked, "So how is Hugh? I know he's based in New York. Oh, count on it. You, too." He glanced down at her, his bottom lip between his teeth as he listened. "Yes, well, the thing is, Tom, I'm getting married in a few weeks and I'd really like you to be there, if possible."

Renee raised onto her toes and kissed his chin. Then she extricated herself, gave a fake shiver to explain her leaving and hurried back inside. Tears were rolling down her cheeks and she hastily brushed them away as she approached the table and slumped into her chair. She sniffled, laughing at herself as she did.

"What's wrong?" Clay demanded, half rising, ready to fix things.

Renee waved him back down. "Absolutely nothing, my friend. Not one thing. Everything's gonna be just fine." She sighed as she looked around her at the expressions of concern. "You guys want to come to a jumped up wedding?"

Vanessa's mouth dropped open. "Omigod. Are you pregnant?"

Renee threw back her head and laughed. "No, but that can be remedied!"

Epilogue

Florida weather proved more fickle than Mark expected as the hand of winter swept far enough south to reach Renee's parents' place in Destin. The chapel at Grace Church glowed with warmth, filled as it was with love, candlelight and colorful fall blooms.

Two days earlier, Mark had experienced his first Thanksgiving and was now attending his first wedding.

He wore a gray tuxedo, content to have ditched the black he had become so accustomed to in the past. In fact he had ditched the past entirely. This is what his parents would have wanted for him, Mark thought, as he waited at the altar for his bride to appear. He felt they were with him in spirit on his day of days.

For a brief moment, he thought of Corbett Lazlo and wished he had been free to come. But their association was over and he'd probably never see the man again.

Then he forgot everything but Renee as she appeared at the end of the aisle on her father's arm. Her steps were slow and measured, so unlike her usual energetic stride, he almost laughed. How beautifully she fit the role of bride, calm and serene and so very elegant.

His darling had chosen white lace, a close-fitting gown that modeled her perfect figure. A simple mantilla draped her sleek, dark hair. She wore her mother's wedding dress. The lovely Mrs. Leblanc would probably still fit into it herself, he thought, sending her a smile. He imagined Renee would be the image of her mum in twenty years, still a beauty.

Renee's father had tears in his eyes as he approached the altar to give her away. Who could blame the man? She was such a treasure.

Later, at the reception, a speedily arranged yet rather grand affair that overtook a ballroom in the local Marriott, Mark promised her dad he would take excellent care of her.

"Well, that will make you the first," the old fellow told him. "She would never let anyone else do it, so good luck!" He winked and slapped Mark on the back. "Watch out she doesn't call all the shots."

Renee had approached and overheard that

warning. She leaned forward and said to her father in a stage whisper, "The trick is to let him *think* he's the boss! I learned that from my mama."

Mark laughed along with everyone else, though he suspected she was half serious. He didn't mind. She cared, that was all that mattered. She loved him.

They danced, gazes locked, sharing happiness he had never dared dream he would ever feel.

The Merciers, the Senates and the Michaelses, along with several more of Renee's friends, had flown down for the nuptials. Mark's mates from London and New York had also made the trip, throwing him a bachelor party last evening that had nearly done him in. It still amazed Mark how easily the three of them had resumed the old friendship, as if all those years in between had never happened. They were still *Tomcat*, *Beefcake* and *Sureshot*, the unholy triumvirate.

"You have a phone call!" Tom said, looking puzzled as he handed his cell phone to Mark. "Stop fondling the poor girl and take it, eh? How'd this bloke get my cell number?"

Mark put the phone to his ear, guessing immediately who it was before he answered. He motioned for someone to turn down the music.

"I called to wish you well, Mark," Corbett Lazlo said, his voice clipped as usual. "Please give my regards to your wife."

"Lazlo sends his regards," he told Renee who

wore a worried look. She must be thinking this was a call to duty.

"It's good to hear from you, Corbett," Mark said with feeling. "How is the investigation going?"

Renee grasped his arm and pulled the phone down so that she could hear as well. Mark leaned down so they could listen together.

"You're *not* to worry about that," Lazlo said, sounding stern, much like a father or older brother might. "I have it in hand."

"You've caught Deborah Martine?"

After a short, uncomfortable pause, he added somewhat curtly, "We're working on that. Sonnegut died in his cell. The driver was found dead in his flat. But this is my problem now. You have bigger responsibilities. I want you to let this go, take back your life and be happy, Mark."

"Is that an order, sir?" Mark asked, unable to resist teasing him a bit. Lazlo never unwound, didn't know how. Mark understood, finally, that he had misjudged Corbett and mistaken the man's natural reserve for coldness.

"That's a *definite* order. Your wedding gift will be waiting when you return to Virginia. Make the most of it."

"I can't stand the suspense, Corbett. Will you at least tell us what it is?" He tilted the phone a bit more so Renee could hear better.

"Your real identity has been reestablished," Corbett announced, "complete with your military and SIS performance records. I've sent letters of recommendation and acquired you a sponsor there in the States if you wish to stay."

"'Thank you' seems inadequate," Mark said, swallowing hard and unable to believe the trouble Corbett had gone to on his behalf. "Renee thanks you, too. This means so much to us."

"That's *your* gift. I've sent Renee a convertible. A red one. Godspeed, then," he said and hung up before Mark could reply.

Mark handed the phone back to Tom and frowned down at Renee whose eyes were wide with surprise. "Godspeed, indeed. The way you drive, I'm not at all sure I'll thank him for *that!*"

Renee tiptoed up and kissed him on the lips. "Nobody's perfect, sweetheart. Loving each other's flaws is the trick to making this work."

He lifted her in his arms and whirled her around as the band played on. "You're simply full of all these little *tricks*, aren't you, love?"

She inclined her head toward the nearest exit, hinting it was time to leave the crowd. "Honey, believe me, as far as tricks go, you ain't seen nothin' yet!" She shifted restlessly. "So put me down and let's blow this joint."

"An inappropriate turn of phrase considering our last adventure together," he quipped as he set her on her feet.

Renee kissed him so thoroughly, he forgot where they were.

She broke the kiss when the applause grew louder than the music. Her grin was pure mischief and her whiskey eyes sparkled as they edged toward the door. "Wait till you see the new teddy I'm wearing under this gown. It's *da bomb*."

"I'm ready to detonate right now. Time to evacuate. Run for it!"

They did, hand in hand, under a flurry of birdseed and good wishes. A perfect exit to his old way of life.

* * * * *

SPECIAL EDITION®

LIFE, LOVE AND FAMILY

These contemporary romances will strike a chord with you as heroines juggle life and relationships on their way to true love.

New York Times *bestselling author*
Linda Lael Miller brings you
a BRAND-NEW contemporary story
featuring her fan-favorite
McKettrick family.

Meg McKettrick is surprised to be reunited with her high school flame, Brad O'Ballivan. After enjoying a career as a country-and-western singer, Brad aches for a home and family…and seeing Meg again makes him realize he still loves her. But their pride manages to interfere with love…until an unexpected matchmaker gets involved.

Turn the page for a sneak preview of
THE McKETTRICK WAY
by Linda Lael Miller
On sale November 20
wherever books are sold.

Brad shoved the truck into gear and drove to the bottom of the hill, where the road forked. Turn left, and he'd be home in five minutes. Turn right, and he was headed for Indian Rock.

He had no damn business going to Indian Rock.

He had nothing to say to Meg McKettrick, and if he never set eyes on the woman again, it would be two weeks too soon.

He turned right.

He couldn't have said why.

He just drove straight to the Dixie Dog Drive-In.

Back in the day, he and Meg used to meet at the Dixie Dog, by tacit agreement, when either of them had been away. It had been some kind of universe thing, purely intuitive.

Passing familiar landmarks, Brad told himself he ought to turn around. The old days were gone. Things had ended badly between him and Meg anyhow, and she wasn't going to be at the Dixie Dog.

He kept driving.

He rounded a bend, and there was the Dixie Dog. Its big neon sign, a giant hot dog, was all lit up and going through its corny sequence—first it was covered in red squiggles of light, meant to suggest ketchup, and then yellow, for mustard.

Brad pulled into one of the slots next to a speaker, rolled down the truck window and ordered.

A girl roller-skated out with the order about five minutes later.

When she wheeled up to the driver's window, smiling, her eyes went wide with recognition, and she dropped the tray with a clatter.

Silently Brad swore. Damn if he hadn't forgotten he was a famous country singer.

The girl, a skinny thing wearing too much eye makeup, immediately started to cry. "I'm sorry!" she sobbed, squatting to gather up the mess.

"It's okay," Brad answered quietly, leaning to look down at her, catching a glimpse of her plastic name tag. "It's okay, Mandy. No harm done."

"I'll get you another dog and a shake right away, Mr. O'Ballivan!"

"Mandy?"

She stared up at him pitifully, sniffling. Thanks to the copious tears, most of the goop on her eyes had slid south. "Yes?"

"When you go back inside, could you not mention seeing me?"

"But you're Brad O'Ballivan!"

"Yeah," he answered, suppressing a sigh. "I know."

She rolled a little closer. "You wouldn't happen to have a picture you could autograph for me, would you?"

"Not with me," Brad answered.

"You could sign this napkin, though," Mandy said. "It's only got a little chocolate on the corner."

Brad took the paper napkin and her order pen, and scrawled his name. Handed both items back through the window.

She turned and whizzed back toward the side entrance to the Dixie Dog.

Brad waited, marveling that he hadn't considered incidents like this one before he'd decided to come back home. In retrospect, it seemed shortsighted, to say the least, but the truth was, he'd expected to be—Brad O'Ballivan.

Presently Mandy skated back out again, and this time she managed to hold on to the tray.

"I didn't tell a soul!" she whispered. "But Heather and Darlene *both* asked me why my mascara was all smeared." Efficiently she hooked the tray onto the bottom edge of the window.

Brad extended payment, but Mandy shook her head.

"The boss said it's on the house, since I dumped your first order on the ground."

He smiled. "Okay, then. Thanks."

Mandy retreated, and Brad was just reaching for the food when a bright red Blazer whipped into the space beside his. The driver's door sprang open, crashing into the metal speaker, and somebody got out in a hurry.

Something quickened inside Brad.

And in the next moment Meg McKettrick was standing practically on his running board, her blue eyes blazing.

Brad grinned. "I guess you're not over me after all," he said.

SPECIAL EDITION™

**brings you a heartwarming
new McKettrick's story from**

NEW YORK TIMES BESTSELLING AUTHOR

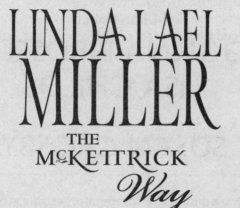

LINDA LAEL MILLER

THE McKETTRICK *Way*

Meg McKettrick is surprised to be reunited
with her high school flame, Brad O'Ballivan,
who has returned home to his family's
neighboring ranch. After seeing Meg again,
Brad realizes he still loves her. But the pride
of both manage to interfere with love...until
an unexpected matchmaker gets involved.

—— McKettrick Women ——

Available December wherever you buy books.

Get ready to meet

THREE WISE WOMEN

with stories by

DONNA BIRDSELL, LISA CHILDS

and

SUSAN CROSBY.

Don't miss these three unforgettable stories about modern-day women and the love and new lives they find on Christmas.

Look for *Three Wise Women*
Available December wherever you buy books.

HARLEQUIN®

The Next Novel.com

HN88147

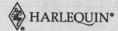

REQUEST YOUR FREE BOOKS!

2 FREE NOVELS PLUS 2 FREE GIFTS!

Silhouette® Romantic

SUSPENSE

Sparked by Danger, Fueled by Passion!

YES! Please send me 2 FREE Silhouette® Romantic Suspense novels and my 2 FREE gifts. After receiving them, if I don't wish to receive any more books, I can return the shipping statement marked "cancel." If I don't cancel, I will receive 4 brand-new novels every month and be billed just $4.24 per book in the U.S., or $4.99 per book in Canada, plus 25¢ shipping and handling per book plus applicable taxes, if any*. That's a savings of at least 15% off the cover price! I understand that accepting the 2 free books and gifts places me under no obligation to buy anything. I can always return a shipment and cancel at any time. Even if I never buy another book from Silhouette, the two free books and gifts are mine to keep forever.

240 SDN EEX6   340 SDN EEYJ

Name	(PLEASE PRINT)	
Address		Apt. #
City	State/Prov.	Zip/Postal Code

Signature (if under 18, a parent or guardian must sign)

Mail to the **Silhouette Reader Service™**:
IN U.S.A.: P.O. Box 1867, Buffalo, NY 14240-1867
IN CANADA: P.O. Box 609, Fort Erie, Ontario L2A 5X3

Not valid to current Silhouette Intimate Moments subscribers.

Want to try two free books from another line?
Call 1-800-873-8635 or visit www.morefreebooks.com.

* Terms and prices subject to change without notice. NY residents add applicable sales tax. Canadian residents will be charged applicable provincial taxes and GST. This offer is limited to one order per household. All orders subject to approval. Credit or debit balances in a customer's account(s) may be offset by any other outstanding balance owed by or to the customer. Please allow 4 to 6 weeks for delivery.

Your Privacy: Silhouette is committed to protecting your privacy. Our Privacy Policy is available online at www.eHarlequin.com or upon request from the Reader Service. From time to time we make our lists of customers available to reputable firms who may have a product or service of interest to you. If you would prefer we not share your name and address, please check here. ☐

SRS07

ATHENA FORCE

Heart-pounding romance and thrilling adventure.

She's their ace in the hole.

Posing as a glamorous high roller, Bethany James, a professional gambler and sometimes government agent, uncovers a mob boss's deadly secrets…and the ugly sins from his past. But when a daredevil with a tantalizing drawl calls her bluff, the stakes—and her heart rate—become much, much higher. Beth can't help but wonder: Have the cards been finally stacked against her?

ATHENA FORCE

Will the women of Athena unravel Arachne's powerful web of blackmail and death…or succumb to their enemies' deadly secrets?

Look for

STACKED DECK

by *Terry Watkins.*

Available December wherever you buy books.

Silhouette® Romantic
SUSPENSE

COMING NEXT MONTH

#1491 HER SWORN PROTECTOR—Marie Ferrarella
The Doctors Pulaski
Cardiologist Kady Pulaski is the only witness to a billionaire shipping magnate's murder. Now the former billionaire's bodyguard, Byron Kennedy, must keep Kady alive long enough to testify against the killer. But can he withstand his attraction to the fiery doctor?

#1492 LAZLO'S LAST STAND—Kathleen Creighton
Mission: Impassioned
When a series of violent attacks afflicts the Lazlo Group, security expert Corbett Lazlo asks Lucia Cordez to play his lover to lure the assassins out of hiding. And as the escalating threat forces them to hole up in intimate quarters, their growing feelings for each other could be an even greater danger.

#1493 DEADLY TEMPTATION—Justine Davis
Redstone, Incorporated
Redstone agent Liana Kiley is stunned to discover that the heroic lawman who saved her life years ago is wanted for corruption...and she's determined to investigate the case. Detective Logan Beck is not happy about dragging Liana back into danger, but with a perfect frame closing in around him, he must put his life—and heart—in her hands.

#1494 THE MEDUSA SEDUCTION—Cindy Dees
The Medusa Project
To catch one of the world's most dangerous terrorists, army captain Brian Riley must abduct and transform civilian Sophie Giovanni into a commando. Sophie is the one woman who can identify Brian's target, but with time running out he must choose between his loyalty to his agency and the woman who's stolen his heart.